"I find this most disturbing," Kasparian said, and it was a memorable understatement.

Sylvie Code, California golden girl no more, lay sprawled on her back, her chest covered with blood. She had apparently been shot, and she was clearly dead. Her face had not been damaged: pale skin, delicate features, a halo of absolutely natural red-gold hair. Sylvie was as gorgeous in death as she had been in life, but Margaret was glad that her carefully made up eyes were closed.

"This is terrible," Margaret said, since understatement seemed to be the order of the day.

"How did it happen? Was it an accident?"

"I have no idea," he answered. "Ah. I understand. You are asking me politely if I shot Sylvie. . . . "

A STUNNING WAY TO DIE

Joyce Christmas

FAWCETT GOLD MEDAL • NEW YORK

A Fawcett Gold Medal Book
Published by Ballantine Books
Copyright © 1991 by Joyce Christmas

Library of Congress Catalog Card Number: 90-93480

ISBN 0-449-14666-9

Manufactured in the United States of America

First Edition: February 1991

For the California Connection:

North: Barry, Carmen, Buddy, and Sam
South: Bob, Steve, Ginger, and Ann
and
Mauro Vincenti,
still pazzo after all these years

Chapter 1

*B*edros *Kasparian* disengaged the alarm on the door of his understated, expensive, and exquisitely tasteful Oriental antiques shop on upper Madison Avenue and entered into darkness faintly scented with sandalwood.

There was not much traffic outside on Madison and few passersby at ten at night. Social New York was still dining or at the theater or at one of the spring season's charity events. The limos that would carry well-dressed bodies home or on to late suppers were idling at curbs while their future passengers ate and drank and repeated fashionable insights they had read in the latest *Vanity Fair* or *Interview* or *Connoisseur*, paraphrased for their own purposes. Ladies shared the latest vile gossip about their dearest friends and eyed one another's gowns, envious or comfortably superior. Some, perhaps, had it in mind to tour the shops tomorrow; a few might choose to stop at Kasparian's place. Even if they did not buy, he was so charming, so gallant in an old-world, old-fashioned way. It was a pleasure simply to sit on the brocade-covered chairs and view a few precious objects from the East while sipping his excellent coffee.

Kasparian touched a switch near the entrance and points of light glowed on the high ceiling. The light caught the gold, plump cheek of a gilded Buddha who had once contemplated centuries of war and peace on a small tropical island off the

1

coast of the Indian subcontinent. The lights illuminated the intricate pattern of threads on a long-dead Rajput maharani's Divali dress displayed on a wall. Here was a deep blue stone set in the handle of a ceremonial dagger; there a fragment of color on a pottery horse that had witnessed the fall of a Chinese emperor. Millions of silken knots tied by tiny Persian and Kashmiri fingers had produced the priceless rugs on the floor of Bedros Kasparian's shop.

He walked through his quiet, rich domain, his safe home after nearly eight tumultuous decades. Once he had scrabbled through garbage heaps in Smyrna, had stolen rotting vegetables in unfriendly Greek villages, had breathed dusty slum air in ancient desert cities. Long ago, he had scraped out a living in Paris and had known the artists who wielded paintbrushes for a pittance but whose work now sold for millions. For a time after the second world war in Europe he had been able to pick up priceless remnants of ruined lives, to sell to eager buyers in America. Then one day he had turned his back on the West and educated himself in the prizes of the ancient East, and had found his final, highly profitable niche in selling rare objects from the Orient.

He was not proud of some of the things he had done to survive and grow wealthy. He was never quite free of reminders that his young man's greed had followed him, even now, into his respectable golden years, when rich society ladies bought his goods and connoisseurs valued his judgment.

Kasparian opened the door at the back of his shop, which led to the room where his perfect merchandise was carefully stored, ready to be displayed piece by piece to acquisitive ladies and gentlemen who trusted that he sold only authentic work. He turned on the light. For a moment he pondered the sight before him, then took one quick step into the room. He scanned the floor, the open shelves where jade and porcelain treasures rested in silk-covered boxes, the bare, serviceable accounts desk with its darkened computer and always ready fax machine. Nothing broken, nothing amiss, nothing to see. He returned to the showroom and picked up the phone on the eighteenth-century Chinese table that served as his personal desk.

He dialed the number of the one person he knew would cope coolly with a sudden dilemma. When Lady Margaret Priam answered, he said, "Margaret, I have a small problem. Do you recall Sylvie Code?"

"Certainly," Lady Margaret said. It was an unlikely question from her employer at an unlikely hour of the night. "She is quite pleasant, considering that she is from California. Divinely beautiful."

"She was exceptionally lovely," Kasparian said. "I wonder if you could arrange to come around to the shop. Immediately."

Margaret had worked with Kasparian for some four years, ever since she had fled from her upper-class English life, and recognized the urgency in his voice.

"Immediately," she said. "Say no more."

Four of the five guests who had come around to Margaret's upper East Side apartment for after-dinner coffee and dessert still offered remarkably intelligent conversation, and everyone was civil and well dressed. Margaret longed to remain with them, but she had not missed Kasparian's use of the past tense in speaking of Sylvie.

"Dears, I have to run out," she told her guests. "Dear Bedros Kasparian seems to be in the midst of a crisis. Be free with anything you find to eat or drink, and I hope to be back before you've departed."

And since they were good friends and knew that Margaret was occasionally involved in unlikely messes, they understood. Her young friend Prince Paul Castrocani halfheartedly offered to accompany her, but he had brought along a lovely and outstandingly wealthy young woman of short acquaintance and he was reluctant to abandon her. Margaret did not stop to change from her at-home attire of silk slacks and shirt but only paused to run a comb through her short blond hair.

Margaret had met Sylvie Code perhaps twice, as Sylvie made quick stops in Manhattan for unspecified business with Kasparian on her way from her Beverly Hills home to points east—London once and then a safari in Kenya. She was a few years younger than Margaret, perhaps about thirty, and married to a very well-to-do Hollywood entertainment-business attorney: the kind of rich, young California matron who could afford Kasparian's prices.

Margaret found a cab at the corner near her apartment and reached the Madison Avenue shop in fifteen minutes.

"Thank you for coming," Kasparian said, and ushered her in with the same graciousness he displayed for his wealthiest customers. "I do not mean to alarm you, but there is something I would like you to see and then to give me advice on how to manage it."

Margaret followed him through the familiar narrow showroom. He appeared to be calm, the same short, elderly man with a bald head fringed in white that Margaret knew from day to day as she assisted in his business. But now his face looked pale and drained.

He pushed open the door to the stockroom.

"I find this most disturbing," he said, and it was a memorable understatement.

Sylvie Code, California golden girl no more, lay sprawled on her back, her chest covered with blood. She had apparently been shot, and she was clearly dead. Her face had not been damaged: pale skin, delicate features, a halo of absolutely natural red-gold hair. Sylvie was as gorgeous in death as she had been in life, but Margaret was glad that her carefully made-up eyes were closed.

"This is terrible," Margaret said, since understatement seemed to be the order of the day. "And that appears to be the weapon." A compact blue-gray gun was lying on the floor near the body.

"Yes," Kasparian said. "It would appear to be."

"How did it happen? Was it an accident?" Margaret was torn between staring at the awful mess on the floor and wanting to observe Kasparian's reaction.

"I have no idea," he answered. "Ah. I understand. You are asking me politely if I shot Sylvie. Mistaking her for an intruder, perhaps?"

"It occurred to me that that might be the case," Margaret said, "and if that is so, we ought not delay in informing the police and making a clean breast of it. Accidents do happen, and I'm sure Sam De Vere would arrange the least possible inconvenience.'' Margaret had no idea if her policeman friend would do any such thing, although he knew and admired Kasparian and would likely behave in a reasonably civilized manner. "He stopped by my place tonight but had to leave on some police business. Perhaps I can catch him. . . .''

"Margaret," Kasparian said gently, "I did not shoot Sylvie. I had no reason to shoot her. We were friends.''

"Well, there it is," Margaret said. "We've gone from surprising an intruder to not having a reason to shoot Sylvie Code." Margaret faced him squarely. "Bedros, you are a dear friend and an excellent employer. As far as I know, you are not murderous by nature. But you had better tell me pretty damned quickly why Sylvie was here instead of at home in Beverly Hills with her husband and what sort of incriminating thing might cause the police to think you killed her.''

Kasparian clasped his hands and paced. "If I say again that I did not kill her, will you believe me?'' He stopped abruptly and faced her. "That is the absolute truth.''

Margaret met his eyes. "I believe you," she told him. Then she ran her hands through her hair. "But I believe there's something rather awful we have to deal with. I recall that no one else has keys to the shop except the security company—and you and me. And I know where my keys are.''

Life in New York City in the last decade of the twentieth century was not as Lady Margaret had expected when she left England and Priam's Priory, the huge pile of stone she called home, with its burdens of history and erratic heating in the winter. It was much more dangerous, if her experience could be trusted. She watched Kasparian pace and prayed that he was not about to be implicated in a violent death.

"Well?'' She waited for Kasparian to suggest who else might have had both the means of access and the inclination to murder. He said nothing.

"I don't like this," she stated finally. "We are ringing De Vere without another moment's delay, and we will work something out.'' She knew that De Vere would not be pleased to learn that Lady Margaret Priam had once again come upon a murder, and it would not matter how strongly she protested that it was absolutely not her fault. Kasparian was a friend, and she had to help. ''And listen to me,'' Margaret said. ''Before the police arrive you will tell me everything, and you won't say anything incriminating to the police.''

''I have nothing to say except the truth,'' Kasparian said. ''I arrived, I turned on the lights, I walked to the back of the shop, and I found Sylvie dead. I called you. I waited. You arrived. That is all.''

Kasparian turned on his heels and went to the telephone. Margaret heard him say, ''An accident. A woman has died suddenly. Yes, thank you. I will be awaiting your people.''

''But that wasn't De Vere,'' Margaret said. ''You should have tried to reach him!''

Kasparian raised his hand to silence her. ''Whatever the consequences of telephoning the police in general, rather than a specific policeman, I wish to avoid the idea that one has something to hide that can be hidden behind friendship. I want no favors.'' He indicated one of the chairs. ''Come, sit down. Sylvie was a very beautiful child, wasn't she?''

Margaret slumped, highly unladylike, in one of the brocade-covered chairs. ''What was she doing here? How did she get in? Who could have shot her? Was it a robber who somehow circumvented the alarms and she surprised him?'' She felt herself becoming more distressed as the implications of the situation became clearer.

Bedros Kasparian smoked only occasionally, and then only a type of Turkish cigarette specially ordered from an old tobacconist who likely was on the brink of going out of business. Now he took one from a case in his desk and smoked it. He watched the stream of bluish smoke rise up into the lights, then he said, ''I suppose I must tell you. She was in the shop because I arranged for her to have the keys. I was to meet her here on business that was very private.''

''Not private any longer,'' Margaret said.

''Private business,'' Kasparian repeated.

Margaret was exasperated. ''You called me to come to

your assistance. You denied knowing Sylvie was in New York. You denied shooting her. And now you claim her arrival was planned and moreover the business was so private you won't tell me." She sat up and leaned forward. "What's up, Bedros?"

"What was up were many millions of dollars," he said after a moment's thought. "And now they have been lost."

Chapter 2

A large number of possibilities proceeded through Margaret's mind, not in an altogether orderly fashion. For one thing, many millions of dollars were not, on some scales, very much at all. Faltering stars of the junk-bond market used to toss about figures far exceeding many millions as though they were dealing with handfuls of scrap paper. Politicians arranged for the mismanagement of sums with far more zeros than a million. People Margaret knew personally spent millions on bits of old carbon. To be sure, they were in the form of diamonds, but nevertheless . . .

"Whose millions?" she asked finally. "And how have they become lost? You'd better explain quickly, or else devote your remaining time to locating your lawyer."

Kasparian seemed hypnotized by the rising smoke from his cigarette. Then he sighed. "You are right, as you often are." He reached again for the phone and dialed. When he spoke, it was evident that he was leaving a message for his lawyer on an answering machine: "I am at the shop and in some difficulty involving a murder. If you cannot reach me, telephone Lady Margaret Priam." He left Margaret's number.

"That's something," Margaret said. "Now talk. Where was Sylvie staying? Did anyone else know she was coming here?"

"She had a number of friends in New York, but I doubt that she would share her business with them. I understood that she was planning to stay at a hotel somewhere in the city."

"The Plaza or the Pierre or the Plaza Athénée or . . . Wait."

Margaret was certain that what she was about to do was unwise, but she did it anyway. She went into the storeroom. The body on the floor seemed more distressing on second viewing. Sylvie's large, luxurious leather handbag lay on the floor a little distance away. Margaret used the edge of her flowing silk shirt to pick it up and nudge open the clasp. A slim wallet, a small makeup case, a comb. A set of keys she recognized as those to Kasparian's shop, capable of neutralizing the alarms and opening the door. A first-class plane ticket showing that she had departed from Los Angeles the day before and was booked to return the day after tomorrow. Nothing else. Margaret was puzzled. No hotel key, no plastic card key to open her room door. Then Margaret lifted out a flimsy bit of paper tucked into a pocket inside the purse. It was a phone-message memo headed "Gladwyn Arms Hotel." Mrs. Code of room 216 had received a message earlier in the day from someone called Peter. She was to call him at the Plaza tomorrow. Margaret replaced the memo and closed the bag. She placed it exactly where she had found it, then returned to Kasparian.

"She seems to have been staying at the last place I would expect," Margaret said. The Gladwyn was a small, unfashionable, and, by New York standards, inexpensive hotel downtown off Park Avenue South. "But someone knew she was there, whoever Peter might be."

"She did not wish to have her presence in the city known," Kasparian said. Then, as an afterthought, "Peter is likely Peter Frost, her husband's law partner." He was beginning to look very drawn and tired.

Margaret was riffling through the pages of the telephone directory. "Oddly enough, there was no hotel key in her bag. Not much of anything, in fact." She found the number she was seeking and dialed. "Messages for Mrs. Code, room two-sixteen, please," she said briskly, suppressing her English accent and summoning up a fairly respectable American voice.

"Margaret!"

She calmed Kasparian with a well-manicured hand. "Thank you," she said as she hung up. "Well! Careless management at that hotel. The desk clerk didn't even ask whether I was she. Now, quickly sum up what Sylvie Code was doing here and how these millions of dollars were lost. The police will be here soon."

"I've known Charles Code since he was a boy here in New York. Indeed, I helped put him through law school. He has done very, very well since moving to California a dozen years ago. I understand that Hollywood lawyers are often more powerful than agents. Sylvie was his second wife. It happens that it was I who introduced them but never with the thought that he would leave his wife to marry her. It was four or five years ago when I happened to be in Los Angeles to visit a friend from the old days. Hugh Lonsdale, the actor. He has since died."

First of all, Margaret was surprised by this offhand mention of an acquaintance with a rather famous person. She remembered seeing Hugh Lonsdale's films as a child and almost falling in love with the sexy, rowdy, and handsome figure who had swashbuckled his way through the Hollywood epics that had enchanted the chilly, heavily rationed postwar British. All the more enchanted because Hugh was an Englishman who had fled to sunny California. He was not quite Errol Flynn, not quite Cary Grant, but still . . . And to think Kasparian had never mentioned knowing him.

Kasparian shook his head. "What was I saying? Sylvie and Charles Code are . . . were divorcing. Sylvie would have received a very substantial share of Charles's assets."

"Millions, in fact?"

"Precisely," Kasparian said. "Sylvie fancied herself in my debt for favors I have done for her. A little money now and then. When the divorce was settled, she was planning to repay me with interest, she said. That is all."

Margaret was not entirely convinced by his story. "*What*

favor? *Why* was she in New York? Bedros, why was she *here* in the middle of the night? Please don't tell me—or the police—that she simply had to see some adorable, old ivory netsukes and couldn't wait until daytime.''

"She wanted to sit down with me to put her indebtedness in writing, in case . . ." He stopped.

"Yes?"

"In the event that something happened to her before she was able to transfer to me what she believed she owed me. She did not want Charles to know that she was here. She did not trust him. It was not a pleasant separation. I might say that they disliked each other intensely by the time divorce was discussed.''

"You are exasperating. That is a terribly flimsy story. Is there no longer a postal service? A telephone on which to discuss details? Is there no fax machine out in the back room of the shop?''

"Sylvie did things her own way," Kasparian said stubbornly. "She wanted to go over her notes with me." Then he added, "She sometimes handcarried very valuable antiques from the West Coast, objects I didn't care to entrust to commercial people. I paid her a commission.''

"This wife of a rich man was in need of money?"

"One cannot have too much," Kasparian answered.

"So you paid her well for her services," Margaret said. "This woman who was to get millions. Well, there are certainly no 'notes' in evidence." She stood up. "Let me think." Then she said with conviction, "It seems simple to me. Her husband did it. If he shoots Sylvie, he keeps everything instead of sharing it in the divorce. Charles Code is the ideal suspect, and you are not.''

"Charles is in Beverly Hills, a continent away."

"Don't make it more difficult," she told him. "We don't know that he is in California. He certainly knows where Sylvie was staying. When I rang the Gladwyn just now I was given a message from him, left at about eight tonight. And there was another message left at about the same time from Iris Metcalfe, of whom you have certainly heard.''

"Social ladies of Mrs. Metcalfe's type are my best customers," Kasparian said carefully. "Naturally I know her. Everyone who follows the activities of New York society knows her. She, too, is an old friend of Sylvie's."

Margaret was thinking hard. "Sylvie's calls came at eight, but she was already gone from her room. A lonely dinner, do you suppose? Or out with one of her New York friends? Or already here and already dead?" Then she asked suddenly, "Do you have the Codes' phone number in California?"

Kasparian pointed to the address book on his desk. As Margaret copied it down, the bell of the shop door rang resoundingly. Kasparian stood up. "The police have arrived and will surely be delighted that a suspect, if not the perfect one, is here to face the music."

Margaret was immensely relieved to see that it was De Vere whom Kasparian admitted.

"You did come after all," she said in a rush. "Bedros refused to ring you personally; he just telephoned the police in general. She was dead when he got here. Of course he didn't do it, but I came right around to help. You do understand that I had to come when he asked. And she was definitely dead. The gun is in there beside the body. . . ."

De Vere stared at Margaret. He looked calm and agreeably attractive, as he had been only hours earlier, wearing his preferred uniform of pressed jeans and sport jacket over a dress shirt, tieless as always.

"I am afraid to ask what you are talking about," De Vere said finally. "I called your apartment to see if the festivities would continue long enough for me to return. Paul said you had rushed out to aid Kasparian in an emergency, so I came to assist. Exactly who has been shot?" He sounded stern. Murder and Margaret was a combination that he had repeatedly (and with some reason) forbidden, although to little avail. Margaret kept coming upon murders.

"It's a young woman who was here to meet with Kasparian. An old friend," she added hastily as De Vere raised an eyebrow. "Truly. Please look before the police get here."

"Margaret, I *am* the police," De Vere said. "Bedros, what kind of trouble have you gotten yourself into?"

"I am perfectly innocent, my boy," Kasparian said. "Margaret seems to feel that trouble may be looming for me, so I have called my lawyer, although I doubt that he knows anything about this sort of business. He specializes in tax matters."

"Come," Margaret said. She led De Vere to the storeroom, but this time she stayed at the door. Kasparian hovered behind her.

De Vere looked down at Sylvie Code's body, at the gun, the handbag, the room. "Nothing disturbed, nothing touched?"

"Nothing," Margaret said, almost too quickly. De Vere didn't appear to notice. "I mean, I came in and looked closely to be sure there was nothing to be done for her."

"And you, Bedros? Did you touch anything?"

"Certainly not. I have seen enough bloody bodies in my time to recognize death without a doubt."

"What an extraordinarily beautiful woman," De Vere said. "I would hate to think that someone who knew her in life could bring himself to destroy that kind of beauty. Any hope it was a robber surprised in the act?"

Margaret said quickly, "Very likely."

Kasparian said, "It is only barely possible that someone got around the alarms." Margaret glared at him, but he paid no heed. "Ah, the rest of the police are at the door, I believe." He hurried away to let them in.

"I don't like this," De Vere said.

"I couldn't refuse to come when he called, could I?" Margaret asked in a pleading attempt to gain a more sympathetic view of her presence. "You know he had nothing to do with shooting her."

De Vere gave her a half smile. He put his arm around her shoulders and drew her close briefly. "I don't like you getting involved," he said, "but what I meant was I don't like this whole situation. He's not behaving right under the circumstances. A little too collected, a little too calm."

"That doesn't make him guilty," she began, but De Vere had gone to join his fellow cops.

After Margaret had been asked what she was doing at the

scene of a murder and had satisfied the detective in charge, the police took Kasparian aside. Eventually there were evidence people, photographers, and a medical examiner to view the remains. A diversion occurred when Kasparian's lawyer arrived. Margaret had been acquainted with Maurice Zahn for almost as long as she had known Bedros, who treated him with a kind of avuncular indulgence that was unlike his normal reserve. Maurice was a tall man in his late fifties, with a distinctive, dark-browed appearance that Margaret found quite attractive. He was reputed to be an excellent lawyer with whom Kasparian entrusted all his affairs.

Margaret turned her back on the gathering in the shop and surreptitiously dialed the Codes' number in Beverly Hills. The man who answered told her that Charles Code was not in, but yes, he would leave a message to call Lady Margaret Priam in New York, no matter what the hour. She did not report to him that Mrs. Code was no more. That would be interfering in police business.

A second call, to Prince Paul Castrocani at her apartment, revealed that while the prince and his delicious date were still there, her other guests had departed.

"We are enjoying a small taste of your fine Napoleon brandy," Paul said. "What is happening?"

"A woman was shot in Kasparian's shop," Margaret said. She heard his anguished sigh. Like De Vere, he did not approve of Margaret mixing with murder. He had shared too many such experiences with her in the past couple of years, always entirely against his will. "Kasparian needed me for moral support. De Vere is here. I will be coming back shortly, but please remain until I get there. If a man called Charles Code telephones me, please, *please*, do your best to determine where he is calling from. He will claim to be in California."

"Claim?"

"For Bedros's sake, I hope Mr. Code is—or was—in New York City today. He's the dead woman's husband, and he is the perfect suspect, except that he was allegedly thousands of miles away from the scene of the crime, while Kasparian was not. Wait for me and take all the brandy you desire. She seems like a nice enough girl.''

''She is rich,'' Paul said, ''but quite without conversation. Perhaps I am maturing.'' Paul sounded dismal, as though by reaching the age of twenty-eight he had begun a downhill slide. ''I wonder if my mother and father had much conversation at first. She did not know Italian when they met and his English remains doubtful to this day.'' Paul's very rich American mother had some years ago abandoned her marriage to his poor but titled Italian father, Prince Aldo Castrocani, leaving behind the decaying villa in Rome to return to her native Texas and another, less dramatic spouse.

''I believe conversation is almost as important as money for an enduring relationship,'' Margaret said. ''I will be with you shortly.''

''You are free to leave,'' De Vere told her.

''Is Kasparian going to be all right? They don't think he did this, do they?''

''Not for me to say,'' De Vere said. ''The police collect the evidence, and someone decides who will be charged. He will not be locked up immediately, if that's what you mean. We will try to determine who murdered this . . . this Mrs. Code, late of Beverly Hills.'' He almost winced at his words. In spite of his long-standing involvement with an aristocratic lady, De Vere was not much enamored of the rich and famous. ''I'll call you tomorrow.''

On her way through the shop she paused to speak to Kasparian. ''You will be all right, then?''

''Yes, yes.'' Kasparian seemed years older than when she had arrived, and somewhat distracted. ''You know Maurice, don't you?''

''Yes, of course. Lovely to see you,'' Margaret said. ''I'm so glad Bedros is in your hands.''

''Perhaps I shall not be representing him, Lady Margaret,'' Maurice said, ''although I am entirely at his service.''

''I don't understand.''

Maurice Zahn hesitated. Then he said, ''Charles Code is my son. He chose to change his name after we had a falling out and he moved away.'' He shrugged as if to suggest that there was no describing what life on the West Coast could do to a man. "Sylvie was my second daughter-in-law. We were not close, but I met her a few times and liked her. I knew that she and Charles were having marital difficulties. I believe she tried to be a good stepmother to my grandchildren, but that life they lead out there . . . ." Maurice shrugged again. Life in Beverly Hills was truly beyond a normal man's comprehension.

"Bedros, you never told me that Maurice and Charles were related." Margaret wondered briefly if a father-in-law would be considered a likely suspect.

"There are many things I have not thought it necessary to tell you," Kasparian said. "This is the least of them."

"Well, yes, of course," Margaret said. "Do you plan to open the shop tomorrow?"

"I think not," Kasparian said. "In fact, I believe I will close for an extended period."

Maurice Zahn nodded. Kasparian seemed to be withdrawing into a remote mental isolation. De Vere was right: He was not behaving like himself.

De Vere followed her to the door. "I'll find you a taxi," he said.

There was a faint misty rain falling. De Vere walked to the curb and peered down Madison to look for an empty taxi. "Margaret, promise that you will keep out of this, even though you are fond of Kasparian."

"You're uneasy about him," Margaret said, and when De Vere nodded, she said firmly, "Kasparian could not have done this awful thing."

"It would be difficult for a person to get into the shop unaided," he replied. "The dead woman may have brought someone with her, but there's no evidence of it. That leaves Kasparian."

"Surely not," Margaret said. "He's never owned a gun, I'm sure. And that gun in there must belong to someone."

A taxi lurched to a stop at De Vere's raised arm.

"All that will be looked into," De Vere said. "We police are not fools."

"And you are the best thing that has happened to me in a

long, long time," Margaret said. "I know you will take care of Bedros."

De Vere grinned and shook his head. "I'll do what I can, but you can't bribe me to alter the facts, even with a pledge of lifetime devotion. On the other hand, could we go away somewhere next weekend? I can manage a couple of days. There's a nice old inn upstate. . . ."

Margaret evaded a definite answer. De Vere had so little free time that it pained her to refuse a few days together that would have delighted her.

"I'd adore to, but . . ." She didn't want to say that something might come up about Kasparian, that she might be needed. Then she pushed her guilt aside and said, "I can't. I have to stand by Bedros. There may be things at the shop to take care of. You do understand, don't you?"

She took De Vere's nod to signify that while he might be disappointed that the weekend had come to nothing, he accepted her decision.

"I'm free almost every evening this week," she said hopefully.

"Okay," he said. "I'd probably have gotten upstate and then been called back for some emergency. This job is beginning to wear me down."

"That's settled," she said, and was relieved that she had not hurt him by her refusal. "I really do owe it to Kasparian."

Indeed, she did owe him something. Not only did the commissions he paid her for working with him enable her to sustain a comfortable life in an expensive city with the aid of her modest inheritance, but a couple of years before Kasparian's gift of a ticket to a charity ball had led to her first meeting with De Vere.

As the taxi sped her homeward, she suddenly sat up straight in the broken-down backseat. Like the dead Sylvie Code, she owed Kasparian a debt that involved a man and a way of life.

The curious coincidence started her thinking again about the husband who had just been saved millions of dollars because a murder had made a divorce unnecessary.

Chapter 3

Margaret arrived home perplexed by the undigested facts and the hordes of possibilities she had acquired in Kasparian's shop.

"The key, the key. Where was Sylvie's hotel-room key?" she asked aloud in the empty elevator that carried her aloft to her far too expensive apartment.

"Why did Iris Metcalfe call Sylvie tonight? An ambitious New York socialite and the wife of an important Hollywood lawyer . . . how are they old friends? Who is this Peter who called? How many others knew she was here?" she murmured as she fitted her several keys into the several locks on her apartment door. It never ceased to amaze her that a building that maintained a phalanx of security guards day and night was still deemed not safe from random intruders who were capable of forcing their way through a steel door into her humble (well, not terribly humble) digs.

"The Gladwyn Arms, Charles Code, millions of dollars, antiques carried from coast to coast. A debt to be repaid," she said aloud as she switched on the lights in her hallway. "A need for money."

"Are you alone, speaking phrases that have no meaning?" Paul's voice came from the darkened living room.

"Ah, Paul. Are *you* alone?"

Prince Paul Castrocani lounged in the dim room, and yes, he was alone.

"My young woman seems to have made a previous engagement for midnight, although I offered to carry her off to any place of her choosing. I do not know what to think of today's women."

Paul was a very handsome young man, of impeccable aristocratic birth on his father's side and good, sound Texas stock (with the added luster of incalculable wealth) on his mother's. If Margaret had been a decade younger, she would not easily have cast him aside for a midnight rendezvous with another. And besides, he was an intelligent, good-humored male, if somewhat misguided in his immediate goals.

"I do not know about today's women myself," Margaret told him. "Especially when one of them gets herself murdered in the storeroom of an antiques shop owned by our friend." She poured herself the end of a bottle of the evening's white wine. "Did Charles Code ring me?"

Paul shook his head. "He is the preferred suspect, you say? And there is a great deal of money involved? Men do not easily surrender their women or their wealth. But if you say he is in California, then the murderer must be the other woman."

"Other woman?" Margaret was thoughtful.

"It seems to me that in America many divorces come about because there is another woman or," he added quickly, "another man. You are certain that Kasparian is not the other man?"

"Oh, certainly not," Margaret said, and then she was not so sure. A divinely beautiful woman can make almost any man a fool for a time. "Not in the way you mean. I do hope he is not charged with the crime. He's an available suspect perhaps, but we can come up with a better one."

"Margaret," Paul said in a warning tone of voice. He had had too much experience with Margaret's pursuit of likely suspects.

"I meant 'we' in general. I won't involve you," she said. "But we know that Kasparian does not murder people."

"We do not know that absolutely," Paul said. "He has a

highly colorful past. If you had paid heed to his tales, you would know that he has managed to survive many unpleasant and even dangerous situations by not altogether socially acceptable means.''

Margaret did not care to think about that. Besides, it all happened long ago, and surely the police were not going to investigate Kasparian's past. She went to the windows that looked upon sparkling towers against a dark sky. The mist formed halos of light around the tallest of the buildings.

''I am thinking now of the debt to Kasparian that Sylvie Code claimed she was going to repay with her millions from the divorce.''

''You did not hear words about this debt from the dead woman but from Kasparian,'' Paul said. ''Indeed, as I understand it, you have only his statement on the reason she was there. Perhaps there was another reason. Perhaps there were no millions, no divorce.''

''Paul, you are absolutely right!'' Margaret turned around to face him. ''The source of my information is only Kasparian. I must talk to him tomorrow. I cannot believe he would lie to me, but under the extreme pressure of such a situation, all things are possible. I wish I could find out what the police are thinking. Could you speak to De Vere?'' Paul and Sam De Vere shared a large apartment in Chelsea owned by Paul's mother, as possibly she owned the entire block on which it was located. One was never surprised by the extent and variety of the holdings of Carolyn Sue Dennis Castrocani Hoopes.

Paul shook his head emphatically. ''You know we seldom overlap in our waking hours, and if by chance we do, I definitely do not discuss his profession, nor does he speak of mine, such as it is.'' Paul was still precariously an employee of United National Bank and Trust, but he had confessed that he felt his days were numbered. The luster of his title and the clout of his stepfather, Benton Hoopes, were not enough, after several years of ineffective financial activity, to assure Paul of a comfortable future as an international banker.

''But if he should mention anything,'' Margaret began.

''He will not. Trust me.''

"I hope he calls."

"De Vere?"

"Charles Code." She paced; she sat; she fidgeted. "Do you know Iris Metcalfe?"

"One does know her," Paul said cautiously. "She is quite a beautiful woman. I do not understand why she chose to marry a man so much shorter than she. But I do not understand anything about what attracts one person to another."

"Money is useful," Margaret said. "You know that, and Horton Metcalfe has pots of it."

"Why do you ask about Mrs. Metcalfe?" Paul asked.

"She is . . . was a friend of Sylvie Code's, and she knew Sylvie was visiting New York although it was supposed to be a secret. Kasparian's word on that again, I'll admit. I must think of a reason for calling on Iris. Aha! I have it!" Margaret went to a sideboard and extracted a pile of papers. "The Hall of Fame."

"I see that I cannot stop you," Paul said, "and I do not wish to participate further in this murder. I am going home to sleep away the sorrow of being abandoned."

Margaret was busily shifting papers. She waved absently as he departed. She found what she was looking for: a nomination form for the Life-style Hall of Fame sponsored by a fashionable New York charity group that had persuaded Lady Margaret to sit on one of its committees. Although Iris Metcalfe's life-style was notably undistinguished except for its conspicuous consumption and lack of intellectual depth, Margaret thought that Iris would welcome a visit from a friend who was eager to nominate her for the honor.

Margaret went to bed feeling that she had accomplished something on Kasparian's behalf.

The phone did not ring until close to two hours later.

"Lady Margaret Priam?" It was a deep male voice, somewhat distorted as though from a great distance. "Charles Code. I apologize for calling so late. I got your message, but then I learned of my . . . of Sylvie's death. I have been on the phone with my father and with the police, who imply that they have determined who likely murdered her. An old acquaintance of my family's. I was shocked."

"Yes," Margaret said, trying to sound bright and fully awake. "Bedros Kasparian. But naturally he could not have done such a thing. It's all a mistake." Then she remembered what she wanted to know from him. "You're calling from Beverly Hills?"

"I had your message from my houseboy," Charles Code said evasively. "I had no idea Sylvie had gone to New York, but, as you know, she had a habit of flying east whenever the spirit moved her."

Margaret did not know any such thing, and she did not call him a liar in spite of his telephone call to his wife at the Gladwyn Arms.

"And when I learned of it," he continued smoothly, "I called her hotel, but she was out. I regret that you and I have not met, but Sylvie spoke of you often. She treasured your great friendship."

Margaret could not imagine how he had believed there was a great friendship between her and Sylvie Code, or what Sylvie might have said to suggest it.

"Our great friendship," Margaret repeated.

"Since you were so close," Charles Code said, "I know you won't refuse me—and Sylvie—one last favor."

"Perhaps," Margaret said cautiously, "if it is possible."

"Please take charge of the details of seeing that the body is flown back here and so forth. I'm not free to come east myself just now. My partner, Peter Frost, is scheduled to arrive in New York tomorrow on business by way of Denver. I'd prefer he had nothing to do with the arrangements unless absolutely necessary. Since you two girls were so close . . ."

Good Lord, Margaret thought. He really does believe that.

"I will do what I can," Margaret said slowly. The idea of going to California and looking Charles Code in the eye had a definite appeal. If he had so many millions, he could surely have hired a killer, if he hadn't done the deed himself. "It is a terrible tragedy, and all the more so because of Bedros's involvement."

"There was no love left between us," Charles Code said. "I might say we'd come to hate each other. As for Bedros, he is a meddler, but I doubt he is capable of murder. I suppose I have to keep up appearances and see that Sylvie is taken care of. Call my office in the morning. My secretary will handle matters on the California end. Just tell her what it's going to cost. There's to be an autopsy, which will take a few days, but I understand the cause of death is obvious, and the weapon was found at the scene. The body will be released by the end of next week. You'll see that she's cremated in New York. I don't want to have people looking at her and moaning about how beautiful she was. We'll have to have some sort of service. A week from Monday, Forest Lawn Cemetery in Glendale. She has a plot there that someone once gave her as a gift.''

"How unusual.''

"An old guy who developed a pathetic passion for her. Wanted to spend eternity with her nearby.'' He sounded disgusted. "At least it's not going to be me. You arrange the details.''

What an awful man, Margaret thought when the conversation concluded. And what a peculiar gift to give a young, beautiful woman. Somehow she was now bound by a nonexistent friendship with a dead woman to arrange her funeral. It was more than enough to make her fly off to California to find a way to prove that Charles Code had murdered his wife.

She tried to return to sleep, but now she could not erase the pictures of Sylvie Code alive—and dead. She wondered about the man who had hated the wife who was divorcing him and taking half his wealth. Would have taken, she corrected herself. How do a man and a woman come to hate each other? A decade before, in her twenties, Margaret had ended an unhappy marriage, but there had been no hate, or so it seemed now. Indeed, on a recent visit to London, she had encountered the man who had once been her husband and had felt a dim pleasure in their hurried (and possibly untruthful) summary of the years since their marriage.

She drowsed. Sleep was returning.

"How beautiful she was. How sad.'' She yawned. "And I am allegedly the victim's best friend. How very odd.''

She had the sense that everyone was holding their breath

in the hope that poor old Bedros Kasparian would hang for the murder of Sylvie Code.

Then she was awake again, scrambling to turn on the light and find a pen in the drawer beside her bed. She was certainly not going to allow that to happen to Kasparian.

"Plane schedules to California," she wrote. "Could Charles have been here and gotten out of town before the body was found?" Then she did sleep, but it was only to awaken to a shock.

Chapter 4

"*Two gentlemen* to see you, Lady Margaret," the tinny voice said through the speaker of her apartment's intercom. "They are from the police."

"Is there a name?" Margaret was barely up and about and had been planning her day.

"No names," the doorman said. "But the IDs look okay. You want me to ask for names?"

"Not necessary," Margaret said. "I know one of them at least." She had already decided to calm her guilty conscience about not immediately sharing her suspicion that Charles Code might have been in New York to shoot his wife, so she was ready to talk. If De Vere was there officially to ask formal questions about Kasparian, he would, of course, follow protocol.

But neither of the two men who presented themselves at her door was De Vere. They looked young, but they did not look friendly.

"Miss Priam, were you a close friend of Sylvie Code?" one asked.

"No," Margaret said. "I was not."

"Several people have stated it," he said.

"You have keys to the shop, right?" asked the other.

She nodded.

"Mrs. Code might have been shot quite early, at seven

o'clock or before. Can anyone testify to your whereabouts at that hour?''

She shook her head.

"What do you know of Bedros Kasparian's financial situation?''

"Nothing. Well, he made money,'' Margaret answered. "Antiques are expensive.'' She was beginning to feel that this was not a friendly meeting. "Are you suggesting that I had something to do with Mrs. Code's murder?''

"We're suggesting nothing, ma'am.''

"I think you are,'' she said. "I had guests at my apartment from about eight. Before that I was here getting ready for them. I made coffee. I whipped cream for a chocolate mousse I had purchased for the occasion—''

"When did you leave Mr. Kasparian's shop yesterday, ma'am? That is, when did you close up?''

"Around six, I suppose. I don't recall precisely. Mr. Kasparian left about five.''

"So you allegedly locked up and turned on the alarms at six?''

"Absolutely.'' Margaret felt herself becoming defensive for no reason. "And I am certain that the alarms were functioning and the doors were locked. Moreover, I did not see Sylvie Code yesterday until I was summoned to the shop by Mr. Kasparian. I intend to make a telephone call now,'' she said coldly. "If that is acceptable.'' She held in check the seething outrage of the innocent party unjustly suspected of a crime. De Vere was still at home when she called.

"What is the official thinking on Kasparian, do you know?'' she asked. "And about me, your close personal friend?''

"I don't know that I can tell you anything,'' De Vere said. "It's not my case.'' He seemed unusually remote. Margaret hoped it was not because she, too, seemed to be under suspicion.

"Aren't those two different things?'' Margaret asked. "Do you mean that you cannot tell because you know nothing, or you will not because you are not permitted to? I only ask because there are two of your people here apparently laboring under the delusion that I might have been involved in Sylvie's murder.''

"We have to look into all possibilities," De Vere said. He did not sound happy. "You were a close friend of the dead woman's.''

"I was *not*!" Margaret said. "I met her twice. Has it occurred to the detectives in charge to investigate whether her husband might have managed to be in New York to shoot her and then catch a plane to somewhere far away in time to respond to calls from the police about her death? He would have been out a pile of money if she had lived to divorce him. Do these policemen know that? And there's also Charles Code's partner, Peter Frost. He was in the city, I am sure. Why not accuse him, rather than me?" Now she could hear the outrage in her voice.

"Please don't be upset," De Vere said. "They are just trying to do their jobs. I know you didn't murder anyone."

"I am going to California, you know," she said firmly. "To attend Sylvie Code's funeral. Is that allowed, or am I to be charged with murder?''

"Of course not," De Vere said. She couldn't tell whether there was any doubt in his voice. "Let me speak to one of the detectives. And then just let them ask their questions. They have to do it.''

The police departed at last, and Margaret's righteous indignation at being a possible suspect subsided. On the other hand, the morning thus far had definitely convinced her that she was going to have to find some answers.

The worst part of dealing with Sylvie Code's murder, as far as Margaret was concerned, was the fact that the most reliable source of information about people like the Codes and Iris Metcalfe and probably anyone who was anyone in Beverly Hills had vanished. Aged society columnist Poppy Dill had performed the rare act of leaving her comfortable apartment to travel abroad. It was an offer that Poppy couldn't refuse: free passage, free food, servants, and free (and luxurious) lodging in the châteaux, town houses, villas, and palaces of old and dear friends across the face of Europe. Margaret was on her own.

Kasparian did not answer the phone in his shop. Maurice Zahn had already departed from his office according to the receptionist, who was not to be tempted into reporting where he had gone, even if she knew.

Iris Metcalfe, however, was in, and willing to take Lady Margaret's call. Iris was so often photographed with her perfect profile to the camera, hands gracefully arranged, legs and feet placed just so, that Margaret could easily accept the rumor of a rumor that she had once been a model. But those days were far behind her now. She was known now as a best-dressed, glamorous hostess, a rich man's wife who pleased the press by being high profile while at the same time having come from nowhere to achieve a position in an exclusive Somewhere. The old rich, of course, couldn't abide her.

"What a surprise!" Iris said. Margaret detected an artificial note to her apparent delight. "I was thinking of you *only* the other day."

"Oh?" Margaret could not imagine any reason Iris had to think of her, ever.

"A lovely dinner party I'm giving next month for Lord and Lady Nutting," Iris said. "They're coming over from England for a few weeks. You must know them. I thought you'd be a perfect addition. Make them feel at home."

"Mmm. I don't have my schedule for next month firmed up as yet," Margaret said. "Do give me a call in a week or two." She did know the Nuttings, who were a ponderously boring couple with a keen—indeed, obsessive—interest in breeds of largish dogs that tended to drool, and in causing game birds to disintegrate at the heft of a shotgun. "Iris, I wondered if I could come around today to discuss a little something."

"Perhaps," Iris said without much enthusiasm. "I'm off to Europe soon, so I have loads of fittings to squeeze in. I have a lunch, of course, and my decorator is coming by today to show me swatches for the new draperies in the library."

"It won't take long," Margaret said. "It's the Life-style Hall of Fame business. They're thinking of you."

"Me?" Iris sounded pleased, silly twit that she was. "Oh, I don't know that I deserve . . ." From the tone of her voice Margaret understood that Iris thought she not only deserved the honor but that it had been damned slow in coming to her.

"Could you make it about eleven?" Iris asked. "That will give us plenty of time and I won't be late to my lunch. It's rather important, or I'd put it off. Do remind me to show you Horton's new prize, a lovely, lovely Renoir I arranged to get for his birthday. He's away this week, or else he'd be right here to show it off to you himself."

"Eleven will be fine," Margaret said. Then she asked, "I say, did you hear about Sylvie Code?"

There was a pause. Iris said, "Heard what?"

"Sylvie was murdered last night."

"How . . . how shocking. I'd forgotten you knew her. Was she mugged? I keep telling Horton that no one is safe in this city."

"Actually she was shot, in Bedros Kasparian's antiques shop."

"Do they know who did it? Surely not that nice old man."

"In his shop, but not by Bedros," Margaret said firmly.

"You must tell me all about it when you come around," Iris said. "I have a call on my other line."

Margaret tried Kasparian's shop again, and this time a woman answered.

"Not in," the woman said.

"It's Lady Margaret Priam. I work with Mr. Kasparian, and I do need to know."

"Ah. This is Bea Zahn," the woman said. "Maurice's wife."

"Yes, of course." Margaret had met her once at an opening of a special exhibit at the shop, a plump, motherly, suburban matron.

"We've decided that Bedros should stay with us until things are settled," Bea told her. "He's been so good to Maurice and me, it's the least we can do. He's in the back room just now, tidying up some business. The police have finished up."

"He could have called me to help," Margaret said.

"Perhaps," Bea said, "but he said something about you being busy trying to figure out who did it." Bea sighed. "He liked Sylvie. Why shoot her? I shouldn't say this, but the person who didn't like her is my son, her husband."

"Charles was in California," Margaret said.

"That is what he told me. He called this morning. But I've lived with lawyers long enough to know that what they say isn't always what they mean. And what's to become of my grandchildren? Alexandra and Dorian, can you believe that? What kind of names are those? Debby, their mother, is making herself a career, so she has no time for them. At least Sylvie tried to see that they were raised right, even if she wasn't . . ." Bea stopped.

"Wasn't what?"

"A motherly type. Look, here's Bedros. You talk to him."

"Margaret," Kasparian said. He sounded totally exhausted. "This is becoming difficult."

"I understand," she said. "And I need to talk with you." She intended to hear his story of divorce and millions and handcarried antiques once more. Paul's remark about Kasparian as her single source of information had not been forgotten. "Will you be in the shop for a time?"

"Yes. Bea is going off to look over Bloomingdale's and Saks. I want to clear up some pending sales since I expect to be away from the shop for some time. We will be leaving for White Plains around three or four."

"I'll be there after I see Iris Metcalfe," Margaret said. "I want to find out how she came to know that Sylvie was in the city, when you said it was a secret."

First things first, however: How to send Sylvie to the spot of land with which her admirer had presented her.

It was easier than Margaret expected to arrange for the final journey of Sylvie Code. All it required was sufficient money and an address on the other end for the receipt of the deceased's ashes by certified mail. Or Margaret could accept the ashes on the husband's behalf and convey them westward herself. And that, she decided, was exactly what she was going to do.

Chapter 5

*S*ince *Iris Metcalfe* fancied herself to be on the cutting edge of both life and style in the New York City of the nineties (aided considerably by her husband's ample fortune), Margaret decided to dress with special care. She had a very nice, businesslike Donna Karan dress she'd recently bought on a day when she was sure that spring would never arrive. It had cheered her up immensely. And her late mother's emerald ring was always impressive. Although Margaret did not especially enjoy engaging in a fashion-and-accessories competition, she wanted to be in a strong position to extract any available information from Iris about Sylvie's visit.

The rosy-brick Metcalfe house was on a little deadend street off Sutton Place in the east fifties. Glossy black shutters opened wide and wrought-iron *faux* balconies graced the windows. Large apartment houses towered over its four stories, but one side of the house had a clear view of the East River and Long Island City on the far bank, as well as a glimpse of the decorative span of the Fifty-ninth Street Bridge.

A maid led her to the library to await Iris. It did not seem to Margaret that the draperies were in need of replacement, but she understood that redecoration was an occupational burden of the well-off woman. As she waited, she scanned the books. There were leather-bound sets on the shelves:

31

Dickens and Thackeray, Shakespeare and every Greek who had ever had a philosophical thought. All were well dusted but few were probably well read. There were also shelves of modern classics: Nancy Reagan's memoirs, Donald Trump's *The Art of the Deal*, Andy Warhol's diaries, and Kendall Smith's *Feathers and Fashion Through History*. She paused before a small pastel hung between two floor-to-ceiling bookcases. It was a dreamy arrangement of flowers, and Margaret suspected that it might be a Redon.

Margaret was leafing through the current issues of *Architectural Digest* when Iris made a grand entrance. The doors to the library were flung open by hands unseen, then Iris Metcalfe glided toward her down a long hallway. Margaret was impressed in spite of herself. As Iris advanced, a good-looking, tallish man with a briefcase crossed the foyer behind her and hastened toward the front door. Then Iris was in the library closing the doors behind her. She approached Margaret with hands graciously outstretched.

"How good of you to come," Iris said. "I've just gotten rid of the decorator fellow. So tiresome to have to see to everything." Iris was very well cared for, a ripe beauty of thirty or so summers who had made an extreme effort to be perfectly put together from head to toe and then some. She was a prize consort for Horton Metcalfe, who was not young but was very distinguished. "Do sit."

Margaret sat at the woman's firm command. Iris was dressed for her important lunch in a simple but obviously expensive dark green tailleur and an ivory satin blouse that complemented her stunning looks: greenish eyes and lustrous dark hair that had been swept back in a vintage chignon. Always the trendsetter. Margaret thought she looked much thinner than she remembered, but a consuming devotion to thinness seemed to be a preoccupation of the lunching ladies. She was also irritatingly nervy, fluttering her hands in purposeless gestures, patting her perfect hair, and crossing and uncrossing her legs. Perhaps it was the result of some substance that cut down on the desire to eat but speeded up the body.

The maid served coffee, then Iris looked at Margaret expectantly. "You mentioned some little formality about this . . . this award."

"The Life-style Hall of Fame." Margaret found the nomination form in her handbag. "We nominators are asked to visit the nominee *in situ,* as it were. I have absolutely no hesitation about recommending you without a glimpse of *any* aspect of your life-style, but I do like to follow the rules." Margaret had seen enough of Iris in passing at parties and charity events to know that she spent a fortune on the clothes aspect of her life-style. On the other hand, the committee ladies were extremely jealous of newcomers like Iris, however exquisitely coiffeured and dressed. Horton Metcalfe was a longtime fixture in high social circles, and people still spoke of his late wife as a treasure untimely snatched from their midst. It took a lot of work for Iris to erase the image of a fortune-hunting climber who had captured a grieving near-saint.

"My life-style . . . well, we do love art. Art is very, very important to us, but simply everyone seems to be into it nowadays," Iris said. "Horty says it's because people think it's a terrific investment and half the people with old masters on their walls couldn't care less. But my computer! That's something else. I don't think any woman in the city has a computer like mine. Horton had a nice little programmer fix me up with special programs so that I know who was to dinner and when, what they ate and what they won't eat, and what I wore and who stopped by for dessert. I do it *all* myself. My wardrobe is all on the computer, too. Now that's Life-style, don't you think? Then because I seem to spend half my life on the telephone arranging things, we have all these phones and lines and buttons. Having a fax is nothing nowadays. Everyone has one, but with mine I can send out the same fax to ten people at once. That's fabulous. Is this what you want to know?"

"I am fascinated," Margaret said.

"Now, about our homes. Besides this place, we have the country place in Connecticut, up near Litchfield. It's a bore getting there, but it's lovely when we do, and the local girls are so grateful to work at the house. Otherwise they wouldn't have a sou to their names.''

Margaret allowed Iris to ramble on, merely blinking as one extravagance followed another. Iris seemed to revel in simply telling about her possessions.

''We have thought about buying a place abroad, but definitely not in the Caribbean. Too many unpredictables, if you know what I mean. We looked at a place in England down the road from one of the RHs—''

''RHs?''

''Royal Highnesses—the Waleses, the Yorks, the queen, and the rest of them. The house was rather grand, but not cozy at all, although RHs make ideal neighbors, as you know.''

''Oh, I do,'' Margaret said, remembering that her brother, the earl, did not get on well with certain RHs of his acquaintance.

''Horty did talk a bit about getting a yacht, but that was back when all those naughty boys were buying them, trying to have a bigger one than the next fellow. Isn't that just like men? A yacht is a terrible responsibility and, to tell the truth, I'm not a good sailor. Oops, I hope that won't count against me.''

''It won't,'' Margaret said. ''Do you ride?''

''A little,'' Iris said cautiously, and by her tone Margaret knew she did not, and was probably terrified of horses.

''I ought to have something about your background,'' Margaret said. She would have coldly stared down a comparative stranger who asked her such a thing, but Iris merely glanced at her quickly and said, ''Good, simple midwestern folks with very fine values and good taste. I believe taste is something you can't suddenly acquire. My mother and father were so refined, although we certainly did not have the kind of money Horton has.''

Margaret decided it was time to get to the point of her visit, now that Iris had been lulled into the dreamy state that occurs when people who have suddenly acquired money get to list their possessions.

"I believe I have all I need," Margaret said. "I suppose you want to know about Sylvie."

"One or two people have called," Iris said. "Terribly shocking. I didn't know her well, you know. They say that Mr. Kasparian shot her."

"I think we will find that he did not do it," Margaret said. "What about the divorce?"

Iris's perfectly contrived makeup could not completely hide the momentary blanch. "Divorce? Those horrible rumors are always following me and Horty around. He *adores* me."

Margaret had a sudden vision of vicious arguments, a tired man of business, however rich, seeking a peaceful evening at home instead of becoming part of a photo opportunity at a gala event; the too-social wife piling up bills; the servants hovering behind doors with their ears to the keyholes, sharing the gossip with the maid next door. The beautiful young wife lured by the excitement of a casual affair from time to time but ever fearful that rumors would reach the husband who paid for the life of luxury.

"I did not mean to suggest a thing about *your* marriage," Margaret said, and tried to sound shocked. "And besides," she added, just a touch maliciously, "I never listen to the gossip. I was referring to Sylvie."

Iris relaxed briefly. "Her. I really didn't know her at all, just the way one does know people one meets, but I'd heard there was some trouble in the marriage. I never dreamed it would come to divorce."

"Or murder."

Iris seemed to find the top row of the farthest bookshelf suddenly fascinating. "Do you mean that Charles Code murdered her? I doubt that. He's quite a nice man, very intelligent, very charming and attractive. But I wouldn't know anything of their private life."

"Yet I understood that Sylvie was often in New York to see you." Margaret decided that she might as well find another best friend for Sylvie Code.

"Oh, no. It was you. . . . " Iris was becoming nervous. The cool facade was not holding up well. "I mean, she used

to call me when she came to Manhattan, but it was to see
you. . . .''

Margaret shook her head. "You know it was not me."

Finally Iris gave up gracefully. "Yes, I know. She said you
were a cover for whatever business she had here. Now I know
absolutely *nothing* about that. She was probably seeing
someone. I know her because we were chums years ago when
we were young and eager. Truly, I seldom saw her of late.
Our lives were very, very different in recent years.'' Iris tried
to convey that she had social position while Sylvie was merely
a California lollipop.

"You rang her at her hotel last evening, when no one was
supposed to know that she was in New York, but she was
not in. Now, if I know that, the police will know it also, and
will probably be around to speak to you.''

The facade crumbled a bit more. "She asked me to call.
Look, I cannot afford to be connected with a scandal,'' Iris
said. "Horton would not tolerate it. She wanted to see me—
today it would have been. She said she wanted to talk about
Charles and that messy divorce. I suppose it was a matter of
needing to talk to a sympathetic friend from the past who
knows you but isn't involved in the immediate problem. In
any case, I've already told the police this. They had no further questions.''

"Exactly how do you happen to know her?'' Margaret
could almost see Iris trying to decide whether to tell her:
Would it sound right for the Life-style Hall of Fame?

"Before I met and married Horton,'' Iris said very reluc-
tantly, "I had some idea that I wanted to be an actress. People told me I was pretty and photogenic and blah, blah, blah.
I made a try in Hollywood, and there actually were a few
lines in a television series and a movie. Sylvie was pursuing
the same impossible pot of gold.'' Iris stretched out her hand
to admire the large diamond on her ring finger: she had found
her pot of gold. "We used to run into each other at parties
and things. During one stretch, when prospects were especially dim, we shared a place for a few months. Then I
couldn't take it. I came east, and there was Horton just wid-
owed and just what I was looking for. Sylvie had met Charles

around the same time, although he was still married, but it turned out all right for her in the end.''

"Except that Sylvie's dead."

"What? Well, yes. There's nothing I can do about that. I hope Mr. Kasparian didn't do it. I've always admired his merchandise. I bought one or two pieces from him during my Oriental phase. It's not the thing just now, is it? Paying all that money for old Japanese things when they're buying up all our new things. Some of my best friends happen to be Japanese, and Horton does a lot of business with them, but all the same . . ." Iris looked at her watch. "Heavens, I'll be late. Is there anything else you need to know for the Hall of Fame?"

"I'll just fill in the form," Margaret told her. "I don't have as much influence as some of the other committee members, but I'll do what I can. It's six months off."

Iris stood up, and the maid appeared with her coat.

"Charles and Sylvie ended up hating each other, didn't they?" Margaret asked.

Iris pursed her lips thoughtfully. "I suppose it was partly because of that Cherylle."

"There was another woman, then?" This sounded promising.

"She was all set to be the next Mrs. Charles Code. Won't she be happy about Sylvie? Of course, Charles will drop her soon enough. She's not much to look at compared to Syl. I'd kill for looks like hers." Iris then had the good sense to say, "You do know what I mean. But she was a schemer, and desperate to have the kind of money I do. She even spoke once about . . ." Iris paused. "I shouldn't say this at all." She contrived to look pained.

"Do tell me," Margaret said.

"She hinted at blackmail once. At first I thought she meant that Mr. Kasparian was blackmailing her. She's known him for a long time. Then," she added too sweetly, "I figured out that it must be the other way around."

Chapter 6

"*I am* going to California on Sunday," Margaret announced to Kasparian. After her visit to Iris Metcalfe, she found him sitting at his desk in the showroom, contemplating a handsome piece of old Koryo porcelain. The deep blue-green pitcher glowed in the light of the desk lamp. Margaret was knowledgeable although not expert about the pieces Kasparian sold, but she knew that Koryo porcelain was especially rare, not only because it was extraordinarily beautiful, but also because it had somehow managed to survive the six centuries since it had been part of the burial accoutrements of a Korean nobleman.

Kasparian looked up. "To what end?"

"Several reasons. I have been cast by Charles Code in the role of Best Friend of the Deceased and possibly Chief Mourner, entirely against my inclination and contrary to reality. More important, I am also among those vaguely suspected of murdering this woman I knew not at all. About that I am merely outraged. I wonder if association with the film business blurs the distinction between fact and fiction." She sat down on the other side of the desk.

Kasparian stroked the delicate curves of the pitcher and said, "I am constantly amazed by the will to survive that beautiful objects seem to have. Think of the troubles, the upheavals, the tragedies, the horrors . . . the mere accidents of daily life. Yet here we see this ancient, breathtaking piece that still lives.''

Margaret said, ''I don't recognize that piece from the inventory. Is it new?''

''Yes. It cost me a considerable sum.'' He stood up and raised the pitcher high above the desk with both hands. ''Look at it,'' he said. ''Amazing, isn't it?''

''Ah!'' Lady Margaret's refined shriek followed the sudden plummet of the pitcher to the polished surface of the desk. Fragments of porcelain flew onto the Oriental carpet and were lost in its design. Kasparian bowed his head over the shards that littered the desk.

''It is all right, my dear,'' Kasparian said. ''It was a fake. Very, very good, but much younger than I and even considerably younger than you.'' He sat down again.

Margaret's rapid heartbeat slowed.

''You were speaking of California,'' he said.

''I spoke with Charles Code last night, very late. He labors under the delusion that Sylvie and I were dear friends. That her frequent visits to New York were in the way of visits to me. Why would Charles and several others think such a thing?'' Margaret watched Kasparian closely.

Kasparian drummed his fingers on the desk and did not meet her eyes. ''I suggested that Sylvie present the idea of you as her friend to her husband. She had business in New York, and she needed a name to give as a reason. She selected yours.''

''She made me her excuse? And you knew? I do not care for that. She knew Iris. Why not use her name?''

''As I understood it—and I do apologize for not telling you—Iris is acquainted with Charles, and as Mrs. Horton Metcalfe she has what might be called a high society profile. Her comings and goings and whereabouts are frequently reported in the press. You, on the other hand, lead a much less publicized life, so your whereabouts are not reported. Then, too, your title enhances your suitability as a friend. It was harmless enough, don't you think?''

''I do not.'' Margaret was annoyed, but whether with Kasparian for not telling her before or with the dead Sylvie for taking such liberties she didn't bother to determine. "In any event, I want to meet Charles Code. I can't get it out of my mind that somehow he had a part in her death, whether in person or viå some other means. He is not a nice man."

"The police don't seem to share your suspicions," Kasparian said wearily. "The detectives in charge—not De Vere, incidentally—implied that they are inclined strongly to my guilt—directly or indirectly. However, they charge me with nothing as yet. Maurice has stood by, and has brought in a nice young lawyer who enjoys criminal matters. At their suggestion, I am remaining reasonably silent."

"Are you feeling well?" she asked suddenly. Kasparian looked small and frail hunched over in his chair.

"It is nothing," he said. "I have worries, even beyond this unfortunate shooting."

"I don't suppose," Margaret said slowly, "that there is any reason why Iris Metcalfe would think that blackmail enters into your relationship with Sylvie."

Kasparian again would not look her in the eyes. He fiddled with one of the porcelain fragments that littered the desk.

"Tell me that you are not concealing something else about this murder," she said. The words were difficult to speak, and she felt a tight knot of fear growing. Kasparian was a kind, lovely man who simply could not be involved in wickedness. "Bedros," she said, "I am very steadfast in my friendships. For better or worse, you can trust me."

He said, almost sadly, "Margaret, I am an old man. My life has not been easy until recent years, although it has always been interesting. I have never done anything with an evil intention. Desperate times, however, sometimes require desperate solutions. Even if they occurred many years in the past, they remain a burden to one's conscience."

He stood up and gazed off into the dim corners of his little world.

"I have not told anyone this," he said, "not even Maurice. A document exists, a kind of diary that was kept for years by a friend now deceased. I mentioned him: Hugh Lonsdale, the film actor. It contains information about an event in my life of which I am not proud. I caused the death of a man who had been a good friend to me. It was not intentional, but it could easily be construed to be otherwise. I would do anything to keep the incident buried forever." He shook his head. "When Hugh's career began to fade, he needed money, so I paid for his silence. Then the diaries fell into Sylvie's hands after Hugh's death a few years ago. She was a young woman who could make her way on her great beauty, but you saw how easily beauty can be smashed by one careless hand. She needed security, she said. Thus I have had occasion to give her money to tide her over when necessary. Charles was not always willing to provide her with everything she felt she needed. In return, she helped with some business matters. I suppose one could say that she held something over me. She always referred to my contributions as loans she would repay with interest, and she had promised to hand over the diaries to me when she no longer needed the security they represented."

"With a profitable divorce upcoming, she felt safe in giving them to you? She was planning to do so last night?" Margaret remembered the sight of Sylvie's body. "But there were no such things when I saw the body. Did you find them when you came upon her? Oh, dear, if the police knew you did, it's a motive: murder her to get back the diaries!"

"No," he said shortly.

"I have it!" Margaret exclaimed. "She brought them with her, and the murderer took them. Wait—the missing hotel-room key. The murderer wanted the diaries, but Sylvie didn't have them, so the murderer took her key, went to her hotel, and searched her room. That means that someone else is now in a position to blackmail you."

Kasparian said slowly, "That is all very logical, except for one thing. I found Sylvie dead somewhat earlier than I let on. It was about eight when I first arrived here and found her. She was dead, just as you saw her, and the diaries were not here, although she had promised to bring them. My first thought was yours: The murderer had taken them. But could I be sure? I found her hotel key, and I went to her room at the hotel. No one stopped me; no one even saw me. I searched the room and found nothing. I left the key in there, shut the door behind me, and made my way back here. At about ten I called you."

"But this is terrible," Margaret said. "If the police find out any of this, they'll certainly believe you shot Sylvie, found the diaries, and destroyed them."

"But I did not," Kasparian said. "Someone else killed her, and someone else has the diaries and is holding on to my fate and the peace of my old age."

"It's got to be Charles," Margaret said. "If not him personally, well, people are often reluctant to do their own evil deeds and money can purchase both a gun and a person to pull the trigger, especially when millions of dollars will be saved. Charles wouldn't care about what you did years and years ago. On the other hand, someone else might find the diaries valuable property. . . ."

"Margaret . . ." Kasparian wandered away into the shadows.

"I am trying to save you, Bedros," she said to his back. "And I am certainly not going to allow you to sit there and be accused of murder. And what about Charles's partner, Peter Frost? We don't know anything about him, but I intend to find out. I have made an appointment to see him this afternoon."

Peter Frost reminded Margaret of one of those ferocious-looking dogs of the snowy north, with his thick grayish-blackish hair and icy pale blue eyes. It seemed to her that there were iron muscles beneath the two-thousand-dollar suit and that a bloody chunk of steak would be his preferred meal.

He had invited her to meet him in a borrowed conference room in the offices of a legal firm located in one of the new glass office towers that seemed to spring up overnight in the east fifties. Margaret was grateful that this appeared to mean a strictly business meeting in the matter of Sylvie Code's death and not a social occasion where two mutual friends of the deceased wept over their memories, especially since Margaret had no memories of Sylvie to speak of.

"A real tragedy," Frost said, and seated her in a leather chair at the end of a vast expanse of polished mahogany.

Although the building was brand new, the interior designer for the offices had managed to create a traditional dark-paneled boardroom with a thick carpet and stiff portraits of the Founders in heavy gold frames. An ornate brass chandelier hung over the center of the conference table. There were no visible windows, but Margaret suspected that behind the cascade of dull bronze drapes was an expanse of glass entirely out of keeping with the subdued, old-fashioned decor.

"I ought to have turned over the details of . . . of the necessities of death to you," Margaret said, "but her husband seemed intent on having me take charge."

"Entirely understandable," he said, "since Charles had gotten wind of what Sylvie and I were planning."

"I'm afraid I don't understand," Margaret said, and was afraid that she did. Ever since she had learned of Peter Frost's call to Sylvie's hotel the night of her murder, she had wondered if there was a relationship between them that went beyond being mere friends by virtue of the two men's business association. "You were . . . very close?" she asked cautiously.

Frost folded his arms and looked off into space toward the end of the oppressively dignified room. Before he could speak, a young, very pretty secretary appeared bearing a tray with a silver tea service and two delicate Wedgwood teacups.

"I took the liberty of asking for tea," he explained. "Just leave it there, sweetheart. We'll serve ourselves." The secretary's tiny grimace at the "sweetheart" went unnoticed by Frost. No doubt that was the way males on the fringes of Hollywood spoke, but Margaret did not think secretaries in high-priced East Coast law firms found it acceptable.

He poured tea for Margaret. "Don't get any mistaken ideas about Syl and me," he said. "She was a real knockout, and that's saying something with Los Angeles crawling with all those gorgeous faces and bodies. But it was strictly business with us. Like any number of people on both coasts, Syl and I did not exactly get along with Charles Code in recent years.'' He shook his head. ''I don't know how he did it, but he did it.''

''It? You mean the murder?''

''Yeah. Charles would try anything if he thought he could get away with it. Of course, it's partly his fault. You would have thought that a smart lawyer would have had her sign an airtight prenuptial agreement, but he's so arrogant he probably thought he could get around community-property laws. I can't imagine he thought the marriage would last forever. So they split, and Sylvie and I had a plan. The divorce would have netted her half of a lot of money and some kind of settlement on the house, which is worth a few million. That's what's happened with Beverly Hills real estate. She was also going to get half of the firm. We were equal if nonspeaking partners. Charles and I only started to make it big around the time they were married, so she could claim it as part of their common assets. I'm making this as simple as I can for you.''

''And I do appreciate it,'' Margaret said.

''Syl would have gotten half of his half of the firm, and then she'd sell out to me, so I'd have three quarters, see? I would have forced him out. Not that I worry about Charles. I saw him moving on to some big executive job at one of the studios, because he's been building a lot of bridges with the money guys here in New York, and he does know how to cut a deal. Most of those guys don't have a clue about making movies. They're real good at redecorating executive offices, though.''

''I see,'' Margaret said. ''So you were in the city last night and telephoned her about a meeting to discuss your business?''

''It was hard for us to meet at the firm. She'd moved in with a friend in Beverly Hills where I didn't care to be seen, so since we were both to be in New York, I made an arrangement with a pal here at Baer Thalmann and Malone to use this room.'' Then he stopped. ''How'd you know about my call? How did you know I was in New York? I told the cops I'd called her from Denver.''

''I surmised that you had arrived because you were already

checked into the Plaza so early. Charles said you were coming from Denver, but I looked at airline schedules and almost no flights come into New York until midday. So you were here when she was murdered.''

"I hope,'' Peter Frost said grimly, "that you are not suggesting that I did it.'' He tensed up, ready to attack.

"Not after what you've just told me,'' Margaret said. "It would be to your advantage that she remain alive. Or so it seems. What I don't understand is why Sylvie apparently had a reason to spend a considerable amount of time in New York. Was it always to meet with you?''

"Not me,'' Peter Frost said. "Oh, once or twice in the past few months, but that was only by chance when we both happened to be here and out of view of our nosy neighbors and colleagues. She might have had some man here on the side.''

"The police seem to think that my friend and employer, Bedros Kasparian, might have done the deed. But he is quite old and not an ideal prospect to be her man on the side.''

Frost said slowly, "Nothing would surprise me, and knowing Sylvie, it could even have been an old guy like this Kasparian.''

"She and Kasparian were not involved in that sort of relationship,'' Margaret said, although she knew no such thing. "What do you mean, 'knowing Sylvie'?''

"She made a sort of specialty of dating older guys, back before Charles. Some women try to find their daddies again. Maybe she was looking for her granddaddy.''

"Older guys like Hugh Lonsdale?'' Margaret asked.

"Now, how would you know about that? Those English scandal sheets?''

"A lucky guess,'' Margaret said, but she did not mention the Lonsdale diaries that had fallen into Sylvie's hands. Nor the unlikely gift of a cemetery plot from an old admirer.

"Anything I can do to help with the arrangements?'' Peter Frost asked. "Shipping a body to the West Coast can't be easy.''

"It's ashes, in any case,'' Margaret said. "On Charles's instructions.''

"Ah." Peter Frost shrugged. "His last cruelty. Hide the beauty she was so proud of."

"There's to be a small graveside service on Monday at that famous cemetery," Margaret said. "I expect to attend. Perhaps you know of others who'd like to be there."

"I'll try to make it," Frost said. "There are plenty of people who'd like a chance to sob at a funeral, as long as there's no actual emotional pain involved."

"I'll be at the Beverly Wilshire," Margaret said.

"Maybe you'll have time to enjoy the most popular sport in town after tennis."

Margaret waited to hear.

"No, wait," he said. "Sex is probably first and tennis second, so shopping would only be third. Some women know every inch of Rodeo Drive as though they built it themselves, brick by gold brick."

With Iris's busy, busy schedule, it was almost a vain hope that Margaret would find her at home near her telephone, admiring her multiple phone lines, buttons, and fax machine. Nevertheless, Margaret dialed her number late in the afternoon after meeting with Peter Frost. Surely Iris, as an old Hollywood chum, would have some idea of Sylvie's relationship with Hugh Lonsdale.

To Margaret's surprise, Iris was actually at home.

"Hugh Lonsdale?" Iris was not blatantly hostile, but the morning's warmth engendered by the possibility of entering the Life-style Hall of Fame had evaporated somewhat. "What about him?"

"I understand that Sylvie had some sort of relationship with him at one time. He gave her certain . . . well, things."

Let us see, Margaret thought, if Iris knows about those infernal diaries.

"Things? I have no idea what you mean. She told me he gave her bits and pieces of junk jewelry, but he was broke by the time she knew him. A dirty old man who used to be a star." Iris's tone indicated that "used to be" was simply not good enough for the likes of her.

"You knew him as well, then?"

"Of course not! I might have seen him once or twice. But he's dead now and I don't know what he has to do with me. Look, Margaret, my decorator has finally gotten here, and I really have to go. Let's have lunch sometime soon." The insincerity of her suggestion was obvious. Margaret hoped it also signaled a withdrawal of the tentative invitation to dine with the Nuttings.

"When I return after Sylvie's funeral next Monday," Margaret said, "I'll ring you."

Chapter 7

M*argaret had* a few days to mull over the murder of
Sylvie Code and make her arrangements to fly west. When
she advised Charles Code's no-nonsense secretary that the
price of her participation in the final journey of Sylvie Code
was a first-class air ticket to Los Angeles and back, there was
no problem.

"Could I speak with Mr. Code?" Margaret asked. "About
the burial . . ."

He was in a meeting, she was told tersely, and not to be
disturbed. Margaret should make all the necessary arrangements.

And that was that.

Although she had never visited Southern California, she
had once visited San Francisco and had been charmed by the
sight of water at every turn and the old Victorian houses and
the astonishing hills and the beautiful Golden Gate Bridge.

"Los Angeles is another story altogether," her friend
Dianne Stark told her, when Margaret sought her out to ask
what to expect. Dianne had once crisscrossed the continent
as a flight attendant before settling down in a contented marriage to a rich New York businessman. "And around Beverly
Hills and Bel-Air and Holmby Hills, everyone looks so
good—tanned and fit and perfectly dressed in elegant-casual

style. The right Maud Frizon shoes, the right Judith Lieber bag, a Chanel blouse, a little Valentino skirt and jacket.''

''Good Lord, whatever shall I wear to the funeral?''

''I doubt you will find the mourners in sober black or navy blue,'' Dianne said. ''You know, I met Sylvie Code at a cocktail party that Iris Metcalfe gave for her a year or so ago. A really gorgeous woman, but not warm. As if she were playing a part and was afraid she'd forget her lines. The husband was there, too.''

''I am most interested in meeting him,'' Margaret said, and wondered if she ever would.

''A nasty piece of work, if you ask me. The kind who keeps looking over your shoulder in case there's someone more important just over the horizon. Condescending, just this side of being rude. Very attractive, though. They made a handsome couple. Is it true that she was murdered by Mr. Kasparian?''

''Are people saying that?'' Margaret did not keep up with the buzz of gossip that occupied many idle women on the social circuit.

''You know how people will talk. That little bit in the papers after it happened got them going. They're saying she and Kasparian were more than friends, but I find that *very* hard to believe.''

Margaret said, ''They are confusing him with someone else.''

Margaret settled on sober navy-blue linen, to show the natives how elegant Easterners dressed for a funeral. She packed sparsely—what she thought was her elegant but casual best for her two-day visit, in case she did manage to venture into the expensive Rodeo Drive shops.

She rang for Kasparian daily and found him increasingly remote.

''No one has tried to contact you about the diaries, then?''

''No, no. She may not have had them with her after all. At least the police have turned their attention to the possibility of a break-in, although I remain under a certain cloud.''

"Kasparian, these objects that Sylvie used to carry for you from the West Coast. What was their source?"

"I have many connections," he said evasively. "I can't go into that."

She did not, therefore, ask him if the fake pitcher derived from Sylvie or one of his many connections.

"About Hugh Lonsdale," she began. "And Sylvie."

"I know nothing," Kasparian said, and that line of questioning was halted.

She decided to put the question to Iris again, but upon ringing the Sutton Place house she was told that Mrs. Metcalfe had departed from the city for a week or two at an exclusive spa where she could not be reached.

Margaret went out one evening with De Vere and mostly avoided talking about the murder except to remark that she still could not imagine how anyone could see either herself or Kasparian as possible murderers.

De Vere tried to sound reassuring. "Don't worry. No one seriously suspects you, and Kasparian has pretty much explained himself—at least for now. It might have been a robber, someone who circumvented the alarms. Or perhaps Kasparian forgot to activate them, or when Mrs. Code entered, she didn't relock the door. Someone might have found a way in unnoticed at the end of the day. Kasparian always has boys around to help out. One of them might have copied the keys and Mrs. Code surprised him. He panicked, shot her, and ran without taking anything. The gun can't be traced so far, but that's not unusual."

"You sound as though you're as eager as I am to find a suspect other than Kasparian—or me," she said. "That's good. I do hope someone is looking into the husband still."

De Vere brushed that aside. "The police look into everything," he said. "Now, I would like to eat my risotto in peace and enjoy your company without mention of murder."

When they parted, she said, "I'll be away only two days. I leave on Sunday and return on Tuesday."

"Don't worry about the old man," De Vere told her. "I won't let anything happen to him, if I can help it."

Prince Paul Castrocani, in effect, said the same thing. "I

will watch and listen," he said, "although I do not care to become too deeply involved in his affairs."

"I hope you'll ring him everyday," Margaret said, "to see how he is holding up." She herself intended to speak to him daily.

"I will telephone him if you wish," Paul said slowly, "but . . ."

"But what?"

"What if he is the murderer?"

"He is not," Margaret said. "I know it. Even the police are hesitant to accuse him." But she was still uneasy. Except for Charles Code, she could not imagine an alternative.

In her comfortable seat in the nearly empty first-class section of the Sunday morning flight from Kennedy airport to the West Coast, Margaret refused the offer of breakfast champagne and toyed with her meal. It appeared to include almost genuine eggs, although someone, somewhere, had a very peculiar notion of what a croissant was supposed to be like. The coffee was quite good, however. The flight attendants in first class were a kindly, nearly middle-aged woman and a curly-haired youth. Both seemed to know that she was Lady Margaret and treated her very well. Neither commented on the compact square box wrapped in brown paper and tied with twine that rested on the empty seat beside her.

It seemed only fitting that the remains of Sylvie Code should fly west in the seating class to which she had become accustomed, even if her trappings were not quite haute couture.

By the time the 747 crossed the Mississippi River thirty-five thousand feet up, Margaret began to slip into a half doze, lulled by the deep and distant throb of the jet engines.

The first thing Margaret noticed on entering from the LAX terminal building was the very blue sky. Then she noticed it was quite a bit warmer than it had been in springtime New York, and there were palm trees.

She chose to find a taxi to take her to the Beverly Wilshire Hotel, having no desire to try to find her way in a rental car along an unfamiliar freeway. In any case, the headlong rush of vehicles going in the opposite direction on the freeway was unnerving. The taxi driver shrugged. People on their way to the beach; by the evening, the stretch of the San Diego Freeway that was taking them from the airport toward the city would be jammed with home-bound beachgoers.

As they sped toward the hotel, Margaret could see the tall buildings of downtown Los Angeles off in the distance, swathed in yellowish-brown haze. As they reached Wilshire Boulevard, the street was lined with new glass-and-concrete office buildings, quite as soulless as an average Manhattan skyscraper. The taxi left her at the Wilshire Boulevard entrance to the hotel, an old building newly polished up, with a jolly row of red and green canopies sheltering the tall windows of what she discovered was the lobby bar.

The bellman took her bag, but she retained Sylvie's ashes in their plain brown wrapper.

"I'll carry this, thank you so much. Lovely."

The lobby was quiet and cool, with a shiny floor of black, red, and cream marble. Elegant white pillars rose to the high ceiling. The faint sound of a piano drifted in, and the young and attractive clerks behind the dark wood reception desk were nicely polite.

"Could you arrange a car for me to rent?" Margaret asked. "And give me directions to a place called Forest Lawn?"

"Glendale? No problem. You can travel by freeway or surface roads, which you might prefer since you are a . . ." The front desk clerk almost said "foreigner." Instead she said, "From out of town."

"Thank you so much," Margaret said.

Margaret set out in a suitably grand car with Sylvie still beside her. The streets were crowded, but the way was eased by periodic traffic lights that enabled her to get her bearings on Santa Monica Boulevard toward Sunset, Hollywood, and Los Feliz boulevards and finally to her destination: a huge green hill capped by a large white building and a simple but gigantic cross.

The administration building inside the iron gates of Forest Lawn was but her first surprise. It was an English Tudor–

style manor house that claimed to be inspired by a place called Compton Wynyates. But surely not, Margaret thought as she entered the reception area where a baronial fireplace held a blazing gas-fed fire. She remembered Compton Wynyates as a turreted fortress of rosy brick set in a hollow somewhere in Warwickshire. But who was she to contradict a beloved, firmly stated fact?

She sat in a tiny room with diamond-shaped window panes where she spoke to a kind man who accepted the ashes of Sylvie Code and the burial certificate issued by the New York funeral director who had overseen the cremation.

He blinked at the cause of death, then said smoothly, "Would you care to see the church and the location of the interment? Near the court of David. No? Well, you will see it tomorrow. Mrs. Code selected the place of rest shortly after her marriage, I understand. She was a great lover of art."

"David? As created by Michelangelo?"

"An exact reproduction."

"I do look forward to the experience," Margaret said. "Tomorrow will be soon enough."

The burial certificate was reviewed again, Sylvie Code was whisked away, and Margaret departed, feeling that her job was one-third done. The next third was to see Sylvie laid to rest, and the last and most important was to see Charles Code in the flesh, to be certain that he was the murderer she believed him to be.

Lady Margaret Priam took a final look at the sturdy Elizabethan manor house where the florist, the mortuary, and the offices of the huge burial park had found their home. It looked in rather better shape than large parts of Priam's Priory did. Perhaps her brother, the earl, ought to hire artisans who seemed to have a way with sixteenth-century buildings. Then she remembered that this place was not from the sixteenth century but the twentieth, and that there was probably a good deal more money to spend on its upkeep than the Priams had.

As she drove away, she noticed that a happy bride and groom were being photographed at the pond across from the

administration building. A plume of spray from the fountain
in the middle created a diverting background. The celebration of a marriage in a burial park struck her as odd in the
extreme, but no less so than finding a Tudor house or a reproduction of David in Southern California.

When she returned to the hotel, she found that someone
named Lulu Lambert, quite unknown to her, had invited her
for drinks at her home in Beverly Hills.

Margaret considered ignoring the call and the invitation.

Then she reconsidered. Someone must have told Lulu
Lambert that Lady Margaret was visiting the city. It could
only be someone connected with Sylvie Code.

Margaret rang Lulu Lambert.

A husky voice sounded not young and not quite grande
dame, but Lulu was commanding.

"We've got to talk," she said. "I need to know about poor
Sylvie." Lulu Lambert's need to know had the same urgency
that Poppy Dill often conveyed, but of course Poppy needed
to know because of her "Social Scene" newspaper column.

"You don't do gossip, do you?" Margaret asked. "As a
professional, for the newspapers. If so, I have nothing to
say."

Lulu Lambert seemed to find that amusing. "Certainly
not. What an idea. Me? A mutual friend told me you were
bringing Sylvie home, and I got the idea you could tell me
what happened."

So Margaret accepted her explicit directions on how to
reach the house, up Canon Drive between two rows of tow-
ering palm trees and then some tricky turns.

"If you get lost," Lulu said, "and if you can find anybody
on these god-blessed streets, you can ask. It's the old Hugh
Lonsdale estate."

The mention of Hugh Lonsdale immediately captured
Margaret's attention.

"It's still called that," Lulu Lambert went on, "even on
the maps they sell of movie-star homes."

"I see," Margaret said. "I'm sure I can find the house."
Then she asked cautiously, "I suppose you've spoken to Bedros Kasparian recently, have you?"

"We keep in touch," Lulu Lambert said. "He told me you'd be at the Wilshire."

"Ah, well, I'll be seeing you shortly then," Margaret said.

Before she departed to meet with Lulu Lambert, Margaret telephoned Kasparian at the Zahns' number.

"Oh, yes, Lady Margaret," Bea Zahn said. "Bedros went back to the city for a couple of days. He had some business. You could try him at the shop, but I'll tell him you called. I'm worried about him, you know. He's been very down, and nothing Maurice and I do helps. I hate to see him this way, he's been so good to us, helping Maurice through law school years back and then Charles. You'll be seeing my grandchildren, so tell them Grandma sends her love. And tell Alexandra that I haven't forgotten her birthday."

"I don't know that I'll be seeing . . . Alexandra and Damian."

"Dorian," Bea corrected, with a hint of disgust.

"And Charles? Is there any message?"

"I've already said what I have to say to him," Bea said. "It seems he only bothers to call his mother when he's lost a wife."

But when Margaret telephoned Kasparian's shop, there was no answer, nor did Kasparian pick up the phone when she dialed his very private home number.

"You have reached . . ." Paul's slightly accented voice on his answering machine indicated that he was either out or still deeply asleep after a long, long Saturday night at the hot clubs of Manhattan. Sometimes, in New York, Margaret became homesick for the English countryside and the massive pile of Priam's Priory where she had spent a tranquil childhood. Today, in sunny Beverly Hills, she was almost feeling homesick for Manhattan.

Chapter 8

*M*argaret *proceeded* north of Sunset Boulevard toward Lulu Lambert's house. She later learned that Nobody who presumed to be Someone lived below Sunset, although the houses she saw seemed quite nice and rather large, albeit crowded onto bitsy pieces of land. Even worse, she later learned, was living south of Wilshire Boulevard.

As she moved upward on roads that were now curving and hilly, many houses were hidden from view by high, thorny hedges or masses of crimson bougainvillea. There was no pavement for idle strollers, and each driveway had a metal sign stuck in the grass that announced proudly and menacingly: ARMED RESPONSE. Not the most welcoming greeting to the innocent Brit expatriate invited to an afternoon cocktail.

Margaret found the street where she had been instructed to make a left turn, and then on the right she saw the imposing ironwork gate that blocked the long drive to the Hugh Lonsdale/Lulu Lambert house. Unlike many houses Margaret had noticed on her travels, this one was not set close to the road but was a considerable distance away. A glimpse of beige stone, an orange tile roof, and oddly shaped chimneys were all that were visible from the street as she tried to find the device that would allow her to make her presence known. Then she heard a buzz and a click and the massive gates swung open.

The drive was lined with squat palms, and there was a veritable jungle of eucalyptus and many unfamiliar growing things beyond. Margaret saw a couple of cozy bungalows hidden among the shrubbery—tangerine rather than the aggressive pink that she had observed to be the color of choice for many buildings in this part of the world.

The house itself was very large, an eclectic concoction that combined Spanish, Moorish, French provincial, and perhaps a hint of Tudor again in a wing that featured more of the diamond-shaped panes that Southern California seemed to think expressed Olde England.

A very proper butler emerged from the arched portico as she drew up, and a Mexican boy appeared to open the car door and then drive her car away to an unseen parking spot.

"Lady Margaret," the butler said. He was portly and balding, with a refined British accent that had been elevated from simple countryman to passable Oxbridge by dint of hard work. "I don't know that you remember me. . . ."

"I'm afraid I . . ." Margaret floundered.

"I worked under Mr. Noakes at Priam's Priory when your late father, the earl, was alive. You were quite young. I recall you used to ride out on your white pony. Madame calls me Millburne now, but I was called Nobby back then."

"Nobby, of course! You dropped the claret when the bishop was dining."

"I was forgiven," Millburne said, "but I see that my sins follow me even here." Then he added glumly, "I am often reminded of the difference between the quality of life at Priam's Priory and . . ." He waved at the semitropical luxury about him.

"I am sure," Margaret said soothingly, "that the money is far, far better here."

"I once thought I might get into films," he said, "but there are few roles for English butlers nowadays." He drew himself up straight. "I am forgetting my place, Lady Margaret. Let me take you in. Mrs. Lambert will be down shortly." He paused. "If you would be so kind as not to mention our connection. . . ."

Margaret nodded, then followed him into the house.

The hall was dim and seemed somewhat threadbare, as if it had not been refurbished since the glory days of Hugh Lonsdale. Millburne showed her into a small Spanish-style room with a red-tiled floor and ornate (and uncomfortable, she found), heavy dark wood chairs with prickly cushions of some primitive woven fabric. Two huge candlesticks with melted white candles stood on either side of a brick fireplace. At least there was no fire on this rather warm day. The door had been left ajar, and Margaret could hear the strains of some peculiar, ethereal music full of whooshes and bells, but whether it was live or recorded she could not determine. It sounded rather New Age and exceedingly odd in this monument to another age.

Since the seats she tried were not pleasant, Margaret roamed about the room. A single small window looked out on an overgrown garden with a dry fountain. She turned to a bookcase with books bound in decaying leather. She was not surprised to find, in this context, that they were mostly dusty (literally) chronicles of Mexican and California history.

She was leafing through a volume on the missions of Southern California when a husky voice at the door said, "Dear Lady Margaret . . ."

Lulu Lambert was ample but perhaps not as massive as her flowing cerise draperies suggested. She was also not young, although her piled-up hair was fervently platinum and her makeup was considerable and colorful.

"I am Lulu Lambert. Welcome to my little home. Come."

The dusty entrance hall, Margaret now saw, was medieval in character. Suits of armor stood in niches, and there were broadswords and crossbows on the walls up near the rafters. There were, however, no snarling mastiffs gnawing at bones in the corners, only a tiny, alert Shih Tzu with a matching cerise bow in its topknot.

On their way to the imposing staircase, preceded by the dog, Margaret caught glimpses of hallways radiating off in several directions—here showing stone latticework recalling princely Indian palaces, there a heavy door with brass fittings from which might emerge a gentleman of Renaissance Florence. A long hall of white arches ended in a row of brilliant red and yellow flowers and a glimpse of sky.

"A most unusual house," Margaret said as they ascended. On the first landing they came upon a stained-glass window that might have been a portrayal of the martyrdom of Saint Catherine, as the kneeling blond figure was surrounded by wheels. On the other hand, it might have been a Beverly Hills matron praying for a Mercedes Benz—the wheeled symbols had a definite kinship to the Mercedes logo.

"Hugh Lonsdale had a broad vision," Lulu said, "closely tied to his most famous roles. The King Arthur thing and the conquistador in Mexico. He loved being the heroic British soldier in India, although I'm sure he never set foot there. In those days they filmed everything right in Hollywood. I've left everything pretty much as I found it when I bought the house. I have a taste for the exotic and the historical. People are always after me to sell, but they want to tear the place down and build anew. That must await my demise, or perhaps a serious state of poverty." Lulu made the latter sound entirely impossible to imagine.

Lulu flung open double doors painted with Boucher-Watteau-Fragonard–style shepherdesses on swings showing off their lacy pantaloons. The dog scampered into a vast room that conveyed an overwhelming impression of boundless white satin.

"Here is my little retreat," Lulu said. "I did redecorate here to suit my personal tastes." The large bed was canopied, with the curtains held in place by plump, naked cupids. There were quite a few mirrors in unexpected places, and the rug was a thick white shag. Lulu led her to an arrangement of chaises and chairs grouped before glass doors that opened onto a tiny balcony. Below, the deep aquamarine water of an irregularly shaped swimming pool was inhabited by a throng of shapely young women in very small bathing costumes. Several others lounged at the pool's edge in earnest intellectual debate with some mature, well-nourished

gentlemen in tennis whites. At a distant table under the shade
of the spreading branches of a venerable tree, a trio of sim-
ilarly clad men appeared to be showing some pretty young
things how to play a card game that provoked considerable
hilarity. There were even a few well-built young men parading their hard-won muscles and sinewy, immortal thighs.
Millburne passed among them, dispensing drinks and gathering up empty glasses.

All very Southern California, Margaret thought, and was
only mildly curious about the elderly woman wearing what
appeared to be a cocktail dress from another era and a flowery garden hat who emerged from the house and sat alone
under an umbrella at one of the poolside tables.

"The children do enjoy Sunday afternoons here," Lulu
said, then plumped herself down on a chaise. "Now, tell me
all about it."

"Sylvie's death? There is little to tell beyond the facts. If
you have spoken to Kasparian recently, you must know all
there is to tell. He found her body. He did not do it, and
neither did I."

"Indeed." Lulu fitted a cigarette into a long holder and
struggled to light it with a jeweled lighter. Her eyesight apparently did not permit a direct hit on the first try. In the
bright afternoon sunlight streaming into the room, she appeared much older than at first viewing. "A good friend is
hard to find these days, Lady Margaret. Sylvie used to say
about you—"

"No," Margaret said. "Enough. I will not continue to be
labeled her friend. I was not. I am not even especially inti-
mate with Kasparian, although I am his friend, and I do feel
a need to help prove him innocent of murder. Perhaps you
ought to tell me of your connection with all this, Sylvie Code
specifically."

Lulu shrugged, a massive undertaking.

"She was a beautiful woman, but I was very disappointed
in how she turned out. She started just as sweet and simple
as could be, fabulous to look at, great body, just enough
conversation to amuse the people who mattered. Marriage
changed her. A life of leisure does these women in. Nothing

to occupy them but shopping and lunching and making trouble."

Margaret understood. It was not very different in similar affluent circles in New York, except that a comfortable life in Manhattan required more umbrellas and fur coats.

"And how is it that you knew her so well?" Margaret asked.

"Oh, people know people around here. I have plenty of room, and I like to help out these kids. Sylvie stayed here for a time before she hooked Charles, and then when the marriage went sour, she moved in again until she could straighten out her life. That was a few months ago."

"I wonder if you would be acquainted with Iris Metcalfe," Margaret said.

"Iris. She used to be named Irene, but she thought Iris was more glamorous. She had a point. Very ambitious, Irene-Iris was."

"She and Sylvie were friends, then?"

"Rivals, I'd say. But little Iris has done very well for herself, don't you think? I try to stay impartial, like to see all my girls do well. Say, is Bedros holding up okay? I didn't like the way he sounded."

"As well as can be expected. I suppose your connection with him is through Hugh Lonsdale."

"In a manner of speaking. Hugh and Bedros knew each other for years. From over there." A wave of her cigarette holder seemed to encompass all the lands on the other side of the Atlantic. "This place is full of things Hugh bought from Bedros when he got busy looting the continent thanks to the war. Couple of wars."

"I understand," Margaret said carefully, "that Mr. Lonsdale was an assiduous diarist."

Lulu struggled upright and leaned forward. "What about the diaries?"

Margaret contrived to look blank. "I know little except that I heard diaries existed," she said. "I thought you might know where they were. Bedros mentioned something. . . ."

"Worth a fortune, if you ask me," Lulu said. "Old Hugh ended up a doddering old fool, but he wrote everything down.

And there was a lot to write, but nothing that isn't done now and a lot worse. When he built this place decades ago, he thought he'd be in clover for the rest of his life. Didn't happen. Spent everything and ended up selling this place to me. I let him live on here, you know, until he died."

"It was said that Sylvie had the diaries, but they seem to be missing," Margaret said.

"Sylvie had 'em, and she was going to give them to Bedros."

"So I understand. But he claims she didn't. We think someone killed her and took the diaries. Who would have wanted to kill Sylvie? Surely someone might have simply paid for them."

"As for wanting to kill Sylvie Code," Lulu said, "that's easy. Charles, certainly, because of the divorce. Cherylle—she's Charles's fancy woman, has plans to marry him. And Debby—that's the ex-wife, who always hated Sylvie. I dunno about Peter Frost, but he'd do anything if it was to his advantage."

"I am looking forward to meeting Charles Code," Margaret said. She suddenly wondered if the missing diaries might be here, in the last place Sylvie had lived. Since she had no reason to trust Lulu Lambert, she didn't want to give her the idea that she could rout out those memories that were, in her words, "worth a fortune."

"I wonder if he'll even show up at the funeral," Lulu said. "Tomorrow at ten, isn't it? I'll be there. Is the murderer going to show up, do you think? That's the way they do it in the movies."

"I believe this is real life," Margaret said, "although they do say life imitates art."

Lulu chuckled. "Especially in this part of the world. Everything gets turned into a high-concept story idea. Stick around for a while and you'll see."

"I am merely passing through," Margaret said, "so I will accept your word." She stood up. The Shih Tzu leaped dangerously from the high bed where it had been snoozing and looked up at Margaret expectantly.

"Don't mind the dog," Lulu said. "He's got a good eye for the girls."

"It might interest you to know," Margaret said, "that beside Kasparian being under some suspicion, the police have decided that I, too, had the opportunity to murder Sylvie."

"Geez, I hate it when the police set their eye on you. Say, I invited you up for cocktails, and I didn't even offer you a drink. Whatever you want. It's in that cabinet. I keep everything handy, drinks and ice, so I don't have to have that stuffed-shirt Millburne around too much."

"I want nothing, I think," Margaret said. "Thank you so much. It's been a tiring day."

"Okay," Lulu said. "I'm glad I had a look at you. Bedros said 'Lady Margaret' and I wondered if you're the real thing."

"Am I?" Margaret asked, and was curious to know whether Lulu Lambert deemed her authentic.

"Oh, sure. No question. You sound enough like Millburne to be his sister."

Margaret suppressed a smile. "I appreciate your support," she said. "I'm sure Millburne would be pleased to know it as well."

"Say, could you pour me a glass of white wine before you go? The French stuff."

Margaret obliged. The "French stuff" was very good wine, indeed. No skimping by Lulu Lambert.

"See you at the church," Lulu said, and chuckled. "Wonder who else will be there. I like a good funeral."

Margaret's phone rang almost as soon as she was in her room at the Beverly Wilshire, ready to take a long bath and call room service.

"Lady Margaret? Charles Code."

"Ah, yes. Everything is arranged. Your wife's ashes are at the mortuary, flowers have been laid on, and the service is at ten."

"Excellent," he said. "By the way, don't pay too much attention to anything Lulu Lambert says. She's an old fool, sitting on top of a fortune in that old house. She hasn't a scrap of sense, and she has a vile tongue in her head."

"How interesting that you should say so," Margaret said. "I really need to rest now, but I will see you tomorrow."

"Mmm," he said noncommittally. "And if you run into my ex-wife, Debby, don't pay any attention to her. She's never gotten over the divorce."

"I doubt that I'll have the opportunity to speak to her," Margaret said.

"Oh, she'll be at the funeral. The only person my ex-wife hates more than me is Sylvie. She'll want to see her safely put away."

Chapter 9

*M*onday, *Sylvie Code's* last day among her friends and enemies, was a glorious, clear day. It was, Margaret supposed, the way Southern California had been when the first film people arrived and saw it as the promised land. The massive cluster of buildings in downtown Los Angeles had shed its smoggy shawl and was as distinct as a photo. Margaret even imagined she saw the glint of the Pacific as she made her way to Forest Lawn.

A stream of cars was entering through the gates, but all those people turned out not to be heading to the Wee Kirk o' the Heather where Sylvie's brief service would take place. Only two cars were parked on the roadway near the little grayish-brown chapel. It was, she had been informed, a faithful reproduction of a famous church in Scotland, associated with Sir Walter Scott, for whom Margaret held an enduring aversion. Nevertheless, nestled among tall trees, with a clipped green lawn at its feet, it was definitely picturesque in the morning light.

Margaret entered the empty chapel. It was small and quite plain but for the stained-glass windows, apparently an abiding decorative feature in this part of the world. To carry out the Scottish ambience, they purported to depict the life and times of Robert Burns's Annie Laurie, an odd choice for a chapel, but perhaps Margaret was forgetting some significant aspect of Annie's history.

A large arrangement of white carnations—Margaret's contribution—stood beside the lectern that faced the pews. All seemed in order, so Margaret went back outside. Another car was parking near the others, and Margaret hoped to see a man who would turn out to be Charles Code emerge from it. It was a man, but surely not Charles. He was tall, indeed willowy, and wore an emerald-green silk shirt, open at the neck, and white linen trousers and jacket. He was deeply tanned, and there were golden highlights in his lush auburn hair, which seemed more likely to be the result of the beautician's artistry rather than nature's. The man did not approach the chapel but rather lounged against his car and managed to look mournful or possibly simply stunned by the early hour.

Margaret withdrew a few steps toward an ivy-covered recess that led to a private garden, reserved, according to a sign, for mourners. She felt that she qualified to a degree and was about to proceed when she heard a man's voice.

"I don't like being pressured," the man said. "I've got enough to worry about."

A woman answered, but she was speaking so softly that it was merely a blur of words.

"She's not stupid," the man said. Then he added, to Margaret's utter astonishment, "Even if she is English."

There was no question now but that Margaret had to know who was hidden away behind the ivy, and who had such a low opinion of the English with only a slightly higher opinion of a particular Englishwoman, perhaps herself.

From where she stood a stone pathway ran parallel to the church, with a low wall beyond which stood a marble statue of Christ, more than slightly reminiscent of the statue that overlooked Rio de Janeiro. She thought she might be able to peer surreptitiously over the wall and catch a glimpse of the couple in the mourners' garden. It was either that or burst in on them in person.

"Lady Margaret!" Lulu Lambert's commanding shout stopped her. Lulu was descending from a stately beige and black Rolls with the aid of a uniformed chauffeur. She was splendidly garbed in flowing pastel chiffon and tiny high-heeled shoes. Her platinum hair seemed to reflect the sunlight. The chauffeur propelled her on her way toward Margaret, then drove the lumbering car around a curve to some remote parking spot. The extraordinary man in white and emerald followed Lulu. Margaret gave a wistful backward glance at the entrance to the garden. Whoever was there would surely not emerge until everyone was safely inside the church, especially if they thought Margaret had overheard any of their words.

"Hell of a day," Lulu said. "Too bad we have to waste it on a funeral. We don't get mornings like this every day of the week."

Margaret was glad to see that a few others were beginning to arrive, although for the life of her she couldn't understand why she felt responsible for a nice turnout at Sylvie's memorial.

"Here's someone you must meet, Lady Margaret," Lulu said as she puffed her way up the curving cement path to the steps of the church. "One of Sylvie's great friends. Come along, Donny, and meet a real lady."

"Donny Bright," the person said. "Enchanted. We have *so* much to talk about."

"I thought I saw Debby as I was coming out of the florist's down by the gate," Lulu said. "I bought a little arrangement for the grave, least I could do."

Donny said, "She's referring to Charles Code's ex-wife, Lady Margaret, in case you don't know all the players in this little drama. Debby is likely absolutely thrilled about Sylvie."

"I've heard of her," Margaret said.

"She's big in real estate now. Nobody better to handle a really important property."

"Not *my* property," Lulu said. "I'd say an ex-wife selling a house to an ex-husband smacks of conflict of interest. And besides, I never liked the idea that she abandoned her children."

Margaret allowed them to chatter on, while keeping an eye

on the entrance to the private garden. So far, no one had appeared.

"Charles could afford them and she couldn't at the time," Donny said. "Don't be mean, Lulu."

"I'm not mean. I like the little girl. Boy's a monster, but it's probably his age. Come along inside. We want a good seat."

"I'm thrilled to meet you at last," Donny said confidentially as Lulu barged ahead.

Margaret braced herself for the legend of the best friend.

"I know all about it," he went on. "The story about being friends and all. It was a necessary part of the glorious design of Sylvie's life. We worked very hard on that."

"Worked? I don't understand."

"I was Sylvie's life-style advisor," Donny said importantly. "Oh, I can tell by your expression that I've confused you. My role. A little of this, a little of that. I used to do strictly hair, but hair is just a tiny part of the whole picture. Taste, the right choices, that's what I provide. Clothes, cars, the house, the decorator, the people to invite, the people definitely not to invite. Servants, restaurants, shops. What's in and what's not. It's all quite important here. Sylvie was one of my prize pupils, and naturally she told me everything."

"Everything?" Margaret wondered if that included incriminating diaries, alleged blackmail, fake Oriental antiques, and anything else that might have led someone to murder her.

"Just about."

Lulu had settled herself in the second pew on the right. Margaret and Donny joined her, but Donny stood to watch the stream of arrivals. Margaret rather hoped that Charles Code would shortly take his place in the front pew as the putative bereaved husband so that she would have him close at hand at the end of the service to ask some pressing questions. For example, had he been speaking to an unknown woman in the garden away from prying eyes?

"There's Debby," Donny announced. "And high drama! Right on her heels is darling Cherylle. They are obviously torn between absolute glee that Sylvie is gone and an intense loathing of one another. There's Peter Frost. I told Sylvie their plan to take the firm right out from under Charles's feet would never work, and I was right."

"Not in the way you meant," Lulu said. "Do you see the children?"

"*I* wouldn't bring children to a funeral," Donny said. "She wasn't even their mother, but then it's only a few words and no ghastly corpse, no last look at the gorgeous face." He paused. "I almost feel a tear coming on, even if she did rather leave me stranded."

"Did she leave something undone, then?"

"In a manner of speaking." Donny sighed. "It's only money. Ah, there's Fuji with the children now. They're coming up to the front to sit in the private seating area off there to the right for the family. He could have brought them in another way instead of parading them. . . ."

An elderly Japanese man was leading two blond children toward the front of the chapel, a boy of ten or eleven and a girl a few years younger.

"Here's Winnie," Donny said. "She's simply swathed in black veils. An awful lot of mourning for someone she loathed, if you ask me."

"Winnie Lonsdale couldn't abide Sylvie," Lulu said. "Hugh Lonsdale's widow. You remember the scandal."

"Not at all, I'm afraid," Margaret said. "Hugh Lonsdale had a widow? I understood him to be . . . to be . . ."

"A ladies' man?" Lulu chuckled. "That he was, up to his dying day. But having a committed wife allowed him to keep having his fun without committing himself, if you get me."

A solemn, robed man had reached the lectern and was shuffling papers. He had the look of a clergyman, although he was wearing rather fancy athletic shoes. Possibly he was planning to get in a few sets of tennis after the service. But so far there was no sign of Charles Code.

"About the scandal," Margaret said.

"Not especially sensational as those things go around here. Sylvie was mixed up in it. Winnie always blamed her for

Hugh's death. The official story is that he died on the tennis court. Well, he was on his last legs. I'm surprised that drink and women hadn't done him in years before.''

"And there's an old friend of yours, Lulu," Donny said suddenly. "The last person I expected to see." He leaned down and whispered a name into Lulu's ear.

She pursed her crimson lips and nodded. "A surprise visitor," she said. "Dropped in out of the blue late last night."

Now Margaret could not resist the impulse to turn to catch a glimpse of the seated attendees. The little church was surprisingly full, but with the exception of Peter Frost, who was standing at the back, and the heavily veiled woman who must be Winnie Lonsdale, she saw no one she knew. Which one, she wondered, was Charles, or had he joined the children in the hidden alcove by some other route? Which was Debby the ex-wife, and which was Cherylle who hoped to be wife-to-be? And which were the two persons she had overheard in the garden?

Then she almost gasped aloud. Surely that was not Kasparian seated far in the back, half hidden by Winnie's veils?

"Lulu," she asked, "is it possible that Bedros is here?"

"Shh," Lulu said. Then she added, "Anything is possible. We'll talk later."

Faint solemn music seeped in from somewhere, but at least there was no chorus of angels or an organ pumping out Bach. The ministerial person cleared his throat, and the rustle and hum of subdued conversation ceased.

Except for Donny, who whispered, "I'm saying a few words since no one else volunteered."

"I would have," Lulu said grumpily, "but Charles forbade me. If he thinks saying no to me is going to improve his chances of buying my house, he's wrong."

"My friends," the clergyman said. "Friends and loved ones of . . .'' He was forced to examine his notes. "Sylvie Code. She was a good friend, beautiful in mind and spirit, a loving mother and wife. . . .'' He recited the formula words, which sounded remarkably lacking in sincerity and apparently did not apply entirely to the late Sylvie Code. In any case, Margaret was too perplexed by the appearance of Kasparian to concentrate on the words.

"Those who would like to say something about the woman to whose memory this service is dedicated . . ." The clergyman looked over his audience hopefully.

Donny stood up and moved to the lectern.

"Sylvie and I had some fabulous times, and we bought some lovely things together. You know you're going to be the center of attention when you're with a beautiful woman like Sylvie. And everybody who knows me knows that's where I like to be."

There was a slight ruffle of chuckles across the aisles. People clearly did know Donny.

"She had her faults," he said, "but I'd like to know who doesn't. That's all forgotten now, and forgiven." He stopped. "Somebody here today probably murdered Sylvie. I think that's really awful."

There was not a sound in the chapel as he sat down. Even the disembodied music ceased abruptly.

"That shook 'em," he said.

"Nobody's going to stand up and confess," Lulu whispered. "It's not a revival meeting, for goodness' sake. But Margaret here will figure it out. I found out she's good at that, and it won't take her long."

Margaret started to protest that she was only staying until the next day, but now the clergyman had returned to the lectern, apparently unsettled by Donny's eulogy.

"Let us . . . let us . . ." he began. "A prayer," he said firmly. "O Lord . . ."

Margaret bowed her head. This was not turning out to be as uncomplicated as she had thought when she set out to confront Charles Code and to clear Kasparian—and herself. The idea that Kasparian had come to California was troubling. Surely he was not a fugitive.

"Amen," the clergyman said with considerable relief.

Before the echo of the word had evaporated, there was a rush to the door.

"I must see Charles at once," Margaret said.

"He was sitting up in the private section with the children," Donny said. "When I mentioned murder, he was up and away."

"Then I've got to find out what Kasparian is up to," Margaret said. She searched the backs of the departing mourners but did not catch sight of his bald head.

"Not to worry," Lulu said calmly. "He'll be at graveside. He promised."

"You knew he was here?"

"Naturally," Lulu said complacently. "He's staying with me. I haven't actually had a chance to speak to him, but he came in late last night. Someone from the house drove him here this morning, since I had some errands for my driver to do earlier."

Winnie Lonsdale was the only person remaining in her seat.

"Come on, Winnie," Lulu said. "We're off to see her in the ground. Leave your car, Donny, and yours, Lady Margaret. Plenty of room in the Rolls."

Outside in the bright sunshine there were only the four of them left. Kasparian had disappeared, as if he thought he could avoid Margaret forever.

"Winnie, this is Lady Margaret Priam," Lulu said. The woman pushed back her veils and Margaret looked into old, sad, slightly crazed eyes.

"A friend of that evil woman," Winnie said. "Nobody happier than me to see her dead."

"Now, now, Winnie," Donny said. "People will think you're not all there if you keep on that way."

"I only speak the truth," Winnie said.

Lulu peered up and down the hilly roadway. "Where is that man with my car?"

She started across the road to where Margaret and Donny had parked. The rest of them followed, and none of them took notice of the black car that glided out of a drive that wound behind the church and disappeared into the deep woods.

Only when its engine roared and it headed directly at the group in the middle of the road did the quartet of heads jerk around. Donny grabbed Lulu and Winnie and pulled them out of its path, while Margaret made an agile leap that took her out of danger, although she felt the rush of air and the heat of the car as it passed close to her.

"Give me a break," Donny said. "That is not acceptable behavior."

"Could you see who it was?" Margaret was breathing hard. The car was racing down the hill toward the entrance gates, passing between the hills lined with memorial tablets sunk into the turf.

"Tinted windows," Donny said. "Some kind of lunatic." His eyes met Margaret's, and they silently shared their doubt that it was some kind of random crazed person. "Charles has a car like it," he said softly, for Margaret's ears only. "Rather like it, at least."

"There's my car," Lulu said. "Nearly had the life scared out of me."

"Can't kill me that easily," Winnie said, adjusting her veils.

"Nobody's trying to kill you, Winnie," Lulu said. "Get in and forget it."

"I believe I'll drive myself after all," Margaret said. "I'll meet you at the interment site."

Margaret drove slowly past the hundreds and hundreds of graves on the sloping hillsides. A few had flowers from recent burials, but mostly the place looked like a big, peaceful park.

She was convinced that the speeding car had not been driven by a crazed person who simply wanted to demolish whoever stood in the way. It had been intentional: if not to kill, then at least to frighten one or another or all of them. But surely Charles Code was too smart to commit murder publicly in a cemetery. She was curious to see who would not be at the graveside.

It turned out that no one was there. The clergyman had arrived, two or three people no one seemed to know, and one or two curious tourists who paused in snapping pictures of the exact reproduction of Michelangelo's David and peering at names on the grave markers. No Charles Code, no

Code children and their Japanese keeper, no ex-wife or current girlfriend. No Peter Frost and no Kasparian.

"Dust to dust," the clergyman intoned somewhat crossly as though he was seriously disappointed at the meager turnout.

"Ashes to ashes," Margaret murmured to herself. She saw again the porcelain pitcher that had smashed to bits on Kasparian's desk.

She was relieved to discover that somewhere along the way she had decided that she would stay on for a day or two to see if she could figure out who had tried to kill one or all of the last four people to leave the church.

The graveside words were soon finished.

"I'm heading home," Lulu said. "Come on, Winnie."

But Winnie was straying among the plaques set in the lush turf. She stopped for a moment near Sylvie's little spot in the earth and stared down at it. She shook her head and then followed Lulu, trailing clouds of black veiling.

"Lady Margaret," Donny said, "we have to do lunch. There are a few things we ought to discuss. Put all our bad thoughts in the proper perspective."

"What bad thoughts would those be?"

Donny shrugged. "It's pretty obvious, isn't it? The killing isn't over. Whoever did Sylvie in is around waiting to finish one of us off. Polo Lounge at the Beverly Hills at one-thirty. I have some things to do."

Donny slipped into the Rolls after Lulu and Winnie, and the car glided away, down the hill.

Margaret walked over to the spot where Winnie had paused.

The marker in the ground read: HUGH LONSDALE, ACTOR.

Chapter 10

In the couple of hours before she was to meet Donny Bright, Margaret had a choice. She could proceed at once to Lulu Lambert's house and find out exactly what Kasparian was doing in California. Or she could seek out Charles Code at home in Beverly Hills. If he was not there, she thought she might have a word with Cherylle, whom she understood had taken up permanent residence. She might find a black car with tinted windows among the Code selection of automobiles. She chose the Charles Code option.

She drove back along the crowded boulevards, past older but prosperous residential neighborhoods, garish fast-food spots and heavily patronized gas stations, tall apartment buildings and occasional stunning renovations that had turned decaying Art Deco and Moderne buildings into bright new re-creations of the past. To her right loomed the hills of Hollywood with houses clinging improbably to the sides of cliffs. One grand tremor, she thought, and that precarious world would come tumbling down. She drove into Beverly Hills on Santa Monica Boulevard and turned right when she saw a street with the dramatic stands of palms on either side that signaled the way into the land of the rich and famous.

Although she was without directions, and had merely reviewed a map to match the Code address with a likely road, she was nevertheless confident that she would reach her goal.

These clean, quiet streets had a way of inducing some superwoman assurance that all must go well. Now and then a very expensive auto passed her heading in the opposite direction, mostly driven by glossy women whom she imagined were intent on reaching the expensive shops on and around Rodeo Drive or hairstyling appointments or meetings with girlfriends for lunch or lovers for dalliance.

On this venture into the depths of Beverly Hills, however, her confidence was briefly foiled. She found herself lost on the hilly streets. Masses of scarlet and orange bougainvillea and trailing ivy hid street names and numbers, if they even existed. Tall Italian cypresses rose above vine-covered walls, and through gates and beyond foliage she glimpsed a wild variety of domestic architecture: classical Greek columns fronting a mansion; stucco and wood re-creating an impossibly huge Normandy farmhouse; a Palladian fantasy; a modernistic pile of gleaming white stone, metal, and glass.

She finally stopped at the roadside and found her map.

"Ma'am?" A very handsome young man in a light brown police officer's uniform leaned in toward her window. The patrol car had pulled up quietly behind her.

"Oh, lovely!" Margaret said. "I seem to be hopelessly lost."

"Just what are you looking for? We kinda discourage people from hanging around the neighborhood," the young man said. His smile represented a considerable expenditure in important cosmetic dentistry.

"I *do* understand," Margaret said. "Very wise. I say, could you direct me to Pemberton Drive?"

"I could," he said, "if you can tell me what your business is."

"I'm visiting an attorney, Charles Code. It's number Twelve Pemberton Drive. I've just attended his wife's funeral. . . . " Then mischief took hold of Margaret's brain and, alas, her tongue. "I am investigating her murder."

The police officer's eyes narrowed. "Wait a minute," he said. "It's television, right? You're filming. Where's the crew?" He looked around quickly, as though expecting to see a director and cameramen. Seeing nothing of the sort, he turned a bit more serious.

"No, no," Margaret said. "It's real life." She was sorry now that she had allowed a momentary impulse to confuse the situation. If anything, the policeman was more convinced than ever that she was up to something nefarious. "I'm sorry. It's that I am terribly upset. She was shot. Back in New York. She was a dear friend. . . . " Margaret suddenly realized how easy it was to make Sylvie Code into her best friend in the world, just like that. "I . . . I . . ." She tried for a hint of hysteria, a touching tear.

Something must have worked because the policeman said, "If you'll follow us, we'll show you the way. It's not that easy to find."

A few turns, and the police car drove into a short street unmarked by any sign. Margaret had actually passed it in the course of her search. The handsome policeman saluted as Margaret pulled into the short, curved drive and stopped in front of a facade that appeared to be an attempt at a faithful reproduction of a French château. Two cars were parked in the drive, but neither of them was black.

Margaret rang the doorbell and waited. She noticed that the police car waited outside on the road and drove away only when the old Japanese man she had seen at the service opened the door and admitted her.

"Mr. Code?" she asked.

"Not here," the man said. She thought she saw a sign of recognition. Perhaps he had noticed her at the church. "Missy see you."

He left her standing in an expansive foyer tiled in black and white squares. There were some marble busts set in niches, their grand noses and fleshy chins suggesting that they each might be a French Louis or Charles or some other *roi* of France with many Roman numerals following his name.

"I *definitely* said to call first, but as long as you're here, come on." The woman who approached speaking with an accent of the southern United States was petite and buxom with fluffy honey-colored hair. She wore a transparent robe over a tiny bathing costume. Margaret had glimpsed her at the service and felt certain she was Charles's "fiancée," Cherylle.

"How do you do?" Margaret said, only slightly puzzled by the need to call first. "I'm awfully sorry to trouble you—"

"English, huh? That's good. I told the agency that these damned kiddies are a handful. You English nannies know how to handle 'em."

"I beg your pardon," Margaret said after the retreating Cherylle, who seemed able to make good speed in her high-heeled sandals. Apparently Cherylle thought she was an applicant for the job of caring for the Code children. Margaret's own beloved nanny back home at Priam's Priory had been a sturdy, no-nonsense middle-aged woman who always wore a plain brown dress with a white lace collar and sensible shoes. Modern nannies were rather different, she knew, but she did not imagine that she, in her expensive navy-blue outfit, resembled a nanny in any respect.

"Their stepmother got knocked off," Cherylle said over her shoulder as she led Margaret through a house that shrieked of conspicuous consumption. "They're upset 'cause they liked her and they don't like me much, but the feeling is, let's say, mutual."

They emerged from the house into a square area with a brilliant pool in the center. Cherylle plumped herself down in a comfortably pillowed redwood chair and put out her hand. "You have one of those résumés?"

Instead, Margaret shook the outstretched hand. "How nice to meet you," she said. "I am Lady Margaret Priam, a friend of Sylvie Code's from New York. We didn't have a chance to meet at the service."

Cherylle snatched back her hand from Margaret's as though it were on fire. "You're not from the nanny agency?"

"What an amusing idea," Margaret said.

"Well!" Cherylle pulled her wispy robe around her indignantly and pouted. "You could've told me right away who you were."

"I told you as soon as I had the opportunity," Margaret

said. "I do want to see Mr. Code rather urgently. I missed him at the cemetery, and I understand he's not in now."

"He had to go to his office right after the thing at Forest Lawn," Cherylle said. "He's got this big deal going on, and he didn't have too many tears for old Sylvie. The marriage was finished a long time ago. I've been living here for, like, three months now." A satisfied smile replaced the pout. "Charles and I have serious plans. We're not staying in this place. I didn't mind moving in on a temporary basis, but for long-term the vibrations are out of line. The aura left over from Sylvie was bad enough, but now that she was murdered . . ." Cherylle shuddered. "Anyhow, he's going to build me this really terrific house if we can get the land." She waved a hand that sported rings set with a number of major stones.

"Mrs. Lambert's place?"

"You know an awful lot for a stranger. Oh, I was forgetting. You knew Sylvie."

"Not well," Margaret said firmly. "I arranged to bring her ashes from New York, but it was an act of civilized behavior rather than close friendship."

Cherylle thought about that for half a second, realized that she was out of her depth, and said, "You've got to be a Leo, right?"

"In one life or another," Margaret said. She had little patience with astrological signs except when she agreed with her horoscope.

"Oh, damn, I forgot about the kids. I told Fuji to clean them up and bring them to meet you, but since you're not who you're supposed to be . . ."

"I'd like to meet them anyhow," Margaret said. "I know their grandparents."

"Debby's family?"

"No, Charles's mother and father."

"Them." She sniffed. "He has nothing to do with them. You know, they sent him away to this awful school when he was a kid where they beat him and starved him, and he ran away. And he made it all on his own. He wouldn't even keep their name."

Margaret wondered if Charles had been trying for a faithful reproduction of a half-remembered Dickens novel when he had made up his personal history. Kasparian's aid in sending him through law school appeared to have been forgotten. Instead of contradicting the absent Charles, she merely said, "We sometimes exaggerate points in our past," as Fuji herded the two children from the house. They had changed from their funeral-going clothes into shorts and T-shirts.

"We've got to find a caretaker for those two. The maids don't want the job, and the last nanny quit after a week. Fuji's getting too old, and besides, he's got a lot of other things to do for me around the house. Come on, move it, kiddos," Cherylle said. "This is Lady Margaret from New York and she doesn't have all day."

Dorian, the boy, was sullen. Alexandra looked scared.

"She's not going to bite you," Cherylle said.

"I spoke to your grandmother a few days ago," Margaret said gently. "She said to give you her love, and I promised to do anything I could to make things easier for you. She said to tell Alexandra she hadn't forgotten her birthday."

The two children looked at the ground and fidgeted.

"Sylvie died," the little girl said. "She said I could have a big, big birthday party." She had apparently taken Margaret at her word; the promised party would make things easier for her.

"Alex," Cherylle said firmly, "I told you we'd have a nice birthday for you, but no big party." Cherylle shook her head at Margaret as if to say, "Look what I have to put up with."

"Sylvie promised," Alexandra persisted.

"Charles has got to hand them back to their mother," Cherylle said under her breath, "before they drive me nuts."

"We'll have to see, Alexandra," Margaret said. "I have to go back to New York soon."

"Run along, kids. We'll talk about the birthday thing when I don't have a visitor."

They departed obediently, followed by Fuji.

Cherylle leaned toward Margaret, very chummy now. "I don't know what to do with them. They stayed out of school today because Charles thought it wouldn't look nice if they went. They've got a hundred thousand dollars' worth of toys and dolls and computers. They got their own pool, and they still say they don't have anything to do. I will say this for Sylvie. She got along with them okay, even if she wasn't everybody else's favorite. I wish Charles would give them back to their mother, but I don't think he will.''

"People are very interested in finding out who murdered Sylvie," Margaret said, at last finding an opening to extract information from Cherylle. "Usually the person first suspected would be the estranged husband, but I understand that Mr. Code was at home when she was murdered."

"He didn't do it," Cherylle said. "Some old guy she knew in New York did it, don't ask me why."

"He didn't," Margaret said, "but you're saying that Mr. Code actually was right here with you that night?"

"Well, no. Not exactly. I mean, he was here, he said so, but I was away. I went off to this spa to get in shape, a place near San Diego."

"And how did you decide that you needed to get in shape?" Margaret asked.

"One can always use some toning," Cherylle said. "Charles fixed it up as a surprise. He's really sweet that way, and the whole thing cost, you know, a few thousand bucks."

And by being really sweet, Margaret thought, Charles got his live-in woman out of town so that she wouldn't know if he was in Beverly Hills or far away in New York City when his wife was shot.

Cherylle lowered her voice. "If you're looking for a murderer, you should take a look at Peter Frost. You know about Sylvie and Peter, don't you?"

"Only in very general terms," Margaret said cautiously. Cherylle seemed ready to share confidences.

"They were having an affair. Charles was furious. He was going to divorce her anyhow, but the idea of Peter and Sylvie just about destroyed his serenity, and we'd spent so much time working on that."

"I understood they had a business relationship rather than a romantic one," Margaret said. "Perhaps you could suggest a reason why Peter Frost would shoot her."

Cherylle stood up, flung off her robe, and ran her well-manicured hands over her flat belly and slim hips. "What does it matter now?" she asked. "Dead is dead, and look at all the money Charles saved."

"There is that," Margaret said. She stood up as well. "I'll try to find Charles at his office, but if I miss him, please tell him I'll ring him this evening."

"I'll do that," Cherylle said. She was losing interest in Margaret. She ran her hands through her hair and then became deeply concerned about the state of the polish on the toes of her left foot. "I really have to dress for lunch now," she said. "I'm meeting some friends at the Bistro."

"I, too, have a luncheon engagement," Margaret said.

"We ought to get together again while you're here," Cherylle said with some insincerity.

"Yes," Margaret said. "I'd originally planned to leave tomorrow, but I may stay on. I say, do you drive a black car?"

"Black?" Cherylle wrinkled her pert little nose. "Of course not. I have a darling white Jag that Charles bought for me."

"He does take good care of you," Margaret said.

"It'll be even better when we're married," Cherylle said. "Especially since he doesn't have to give half of everything to Sylvie."

"Very convenient," Margaret said. "Although he's probably learned his lesson now."

"Lesson?"

"Not to marry in haste, and certainly to have a very comprehensive premarital agreement beforehand."

Margaret left Cherylle contemplating those words of wisdom. She found Fuji at the door, waiting to show her out.

"Ah, Mr. . . . Fuji," she began.

"John Fujitsu," he said without a trace of an accent. "I noticed you at the service, but it entirely slipped my mind to mention it to . . . Missy." He seemed to enjoy the fact of his omission.

"You've worked for Mr. Code for some time, then?"

"From the time of his first marriage. I am still here only

because Mrs. Code—Debby—asked me to remain for the sake of the children. Naturally there is other help, but they are unreliable.''

"I don't understand why he gained custody."

"He was in a better position financially to raise them. Debby Code—she calls herself Zahn now, the original name—had pride and ambition, and would not accept more than a small settlement. She is now highly successful and perhaps would take them. I am certainly no longer young enough to supervise them.''

"Mr. Fujitsu," Margaret said, "I believe I must have spoken to you the night Mrs. Code was murdered. I telephoned Charles Code, but he was not in. Do you know where he was? And when he returned?''

John Fujitsu would not meet her eyes. "He telephoned me for his messages. There was a call from you and one from the police in New York. I do not know where he was when he telephoned, and I had retired before he returned. That is to say, I saw him in the course of my duties a day or so later, but I do not know when he returned to this house.''

"I have been wondering," Margaret said carefully, "if he might have been calling from . . . some distant city.''

"That is entirely possible," John Fujitsu said, "but I do not know that.'' It was impossible to read his expression.

"A friend of mine is strongly suspected of murdering Mrs. Code," Margaret said, and wondered if Bedros was actually a fugitive now, hidden away at Lulu Lambert's mansion, or whether he had been granted permission to leave New York. "He did not do it, so I was rather hoping to discover who did.''

"Mrs. Code was not universally popular," he said, "although she had numerous acquaintances. I believe Mr. Bright was correct in his statement that someone at the service murdered her. I, too, find that quite a terrible thought.''

Margaret had a good deal to think about as she made her way past millions and millions of dollars worth of real estate, headed toward the Beverly Hills Hotel and lunch at the Polo Lounge with Donny Bright.

Chapter 11

Here at the Beverly Hills Hotel, pink was definitely the color of choice. That, and a kind of banana-leaf motif in shades of green, which was relentlessly repeated on the wallpaper.

"The Polo Lounge, please." Margaret addressed a passing hotel employee who pointed and Margaret proceeded. She had been given to understand that the Polo Lounge was an important gathering place for the powers in the film business. The casually but well-dressed people being ushered into the low-ceilinged room lined with dark green booths did not look as though they commanded the hearts and minds of the world by way of the movies, but then she had always been surprised to discover that the heads of many major enterprises and financial empires were comparatively ordinary folk. Also evident were a number of very glossy young women with distinguished bosoms and careful makeup, as well as a scattering of well-kept-up older women lunching together. A few of these were emphatically glamorous and vaguely familiar, certainly poised to be photographed at any moment. Margaret imagined that they must be former stars who were hanging on until a publisher thought their memories of Hollywood's golden years and juicy scandals were worth recording via a ghostwriter's word processor.

"Madame?" The correct and imposing maître d' was

skilled, as only a highly competent Italian could be, in treading the very slim line between supercilious doubt that one was who one claimed to be and an appropriate welcome in the event that one actually was as advertised.

"I am to meet Donny Bright for lunch," Margaret said, as grandly as the daughter and sister of a peer of the realm could manage. "Lady Margaret Priam."

"Ah, yes," he said. "A pleasure to have you here. Signor Donny telephoned moments ago. He is slightly delayed and asks that you be seated outside if that is agreeable. Or we can set you in here if you prefer. . . ."

Beyond this room Margaret could see a pleasant patio dining area with greenery and flowers and dappled sun and shade. "Outside would be perfect," she said. "Thank you so much."

She was seated at a table under an umbrella. A glimpse of sky, a large tree spreading shady branches, a hum of conversation. Very pleasant.

"Something to drink, m'lady?" The maître d' hovered. A waiter approached and spoke a few words into his ear. The maître d' said to Margaret, "Champagne is being sent around to you. With the compliments of Mr. Charles Code."

Margaret looked up, startled. "He is here?"

The maître d' signaled the waiter back and spoke quickly in Italian. "Regrettably, m'lady, he has just departed."

She found Charles Code's elusiveness both irritating and suspicious. However, it was excellent champagne.

"Lady Margaret, I am *so* sorry I was delayed." Donny Bright had changed from emerald green and white to shades of beige. He lifted the champagne bottle from the bucket placed beside the table. "Oooh, this is very fine."

"The cost is being borne by Charles Code, who was here."

"And what did the bereaved husband have to say for himself?"

"We failed to meet face-to-face. In fact, I have never met him."

"How did he know it was you then?"

"How, indeed? I spoke my name at the door. Perhaps he

was sitting nearby. Or might he have been lunching with someone who knows me?''

"Well," Donny said slowly, "I can't say that Charles was lunching with her, since I didn't see him at all, but I could swear that that friend of Sylvie's from New York was leaving as I was handing over my car to one of those cute boys who do the parking. Possibly she was with Charles and saw you."

"Who do you mean?"

"The flower lady—Iris."

Margaret's mouth fell open. "You don't mean Iris Metcalfe!"

"Yes, who else? I've met her a few times at the Code place while the marriage was still on. I always thought she was hot for Charles." Donny put up his hands to stop further questions. "No, don't ask me. It's purely idle suspicion. I intuit far too often for my own good. Actually it's a great help in life-style advising. People get the idea that you know what you're talking about. The reason I'm not *absolutely* sure it was Iris is that this woman was wearing a turban—do you think they're coming back? That would be divine. And big shades."

"But Iris . . . I saw her a few days ago. She said nothing about coming to the funeral. In fact, she supposedly had gone off to a spa."

"Very rich people can do things on the spur of the moment," Donny said. "Maybe she thought that now that Charles is comparatively unencumbered, they could develop something steamy. That's another thing rich people can afford to do. Let me just check."

Donny made his way from the patio, pausing from time to time to pat a shoulder, greet a lady, wave to a friend. Working the crowd like the life-style hero he was, Margaret thought. He was soon back.

"Charles was with a woman," he said, "but these people are sufficiently discreet not to be able to remember a thing about her. She couldn't have been a famous client of his, otherwise there would be no doubt about her being named."

"It could have been Iris then?"

"Marginally possible. We'll never know."

But we will, Margaret thought, but did not speak the words aloud.

"The reason I wanted to have lunch," Donny said, "was that we must find out who killed Sylvie."

"I feel the same way," Margaret said, "but I'd like to know your reasons."

"I liked Sylvie, difficult as she could be."

"Not good enough," Margaret said.

"Murder isn't nice," he said.

"Closer, but not there yet," Margaret said.

"I'm mad," Donny said. "First of all, it's very bad for my image when a client is murdered. Then, Syl and I were doing a little business together. She carried stuff by hand from here to New York for that antiques guy. Things he didn't want damaged. I had connections to acquire certain things nobody else could get. We shared the profits. There was a hefty amount due to me when Sylvie was murdered. Not to mention future earnings."

"Illegal things? Genuine? Fake?"

Donny was not terribly discomposed. "A little of this, a little of that. Mostly genuine and legal. She wouldn't have tried to put anything past the old guy. They were friends."

"No drugs or anything like that?"

"Well, I don't know what Sylvie's other business might have been, but I doubt it."

"Did you ever hear rumors of blackmail? Relating to the other business Sylvie might have had?"

That word made Donny nervous. He waved a waiter over and made a considerable fuss about ordering a salad with certain proportions of particular greens. "And bread that's today's vintage, if you don't mind. What would tempt you, Lady Margaret? Everything is good."

Margaret chose a cobb salad with no adjustments.

"Blackmail," she said again.

"What do you know about Sylvie?" he asked. "I know she pretended for Charles's benefit that you were her dear, dear friend, but we know what that was worth."

"I know only what Iris told me," Margaret said. "Aspiring but unsuccessful starlet here in Hollywood. Met Charles

Code who left his wife to marry her. Somehow," she added slowly, "she apparently acquired some diaries that had been written by Hugh Lonsdale. They are said to contain material discrediting, if not worse, to Bedros Kasparian."

"Mr. Kasparian helped her out financially," Donny said. "The diaries may have helped convince him to do so. If that's blackmail."

"She was supposed to be handing them over to him the night she was shot," Margaret told him. "I'm not sure if I should be telling you this, but that's how it was. They were not to be found. Poor Bedros is afraid that whoever took them will expose his past or else try blackmail again."

"Yes," Donny said, "but perhaps the words written down are dangerous to others as well."

"Who?"

"Well, I don't know everything," Donny said defensively. "And I wouldn't dream of spreading gossip. I have my business to consider. All I know is sweet revenge. I won't get my money, but I'll have the pleasure of seeing the one who lost it for me in lots and lots of big trouble. I can only hope it's Charles. He and I definitely did not get along."

"Do you suppose there's any way of finding out whether he really was here in Beverly Hills that night? Or that he definitely was not?"

Donny thought for a moment. "We could ask Fuji."

"No good," Margaret said. "I've already asked. Cherylle was out of town, and Fuji didn't see Charles for a couple of days after the murder, so he doesn't know if he was in Los Angeles or New York or Alaska."

"There's a secretary at Charles's office," Donny said slowly. "I set her straight once on what to do about her hair. She owes me. I could at least find out if he showed at the office the day of the murder, the day after. A definite yes would tell us something; a definite no would tell us a little. Okay, I'll check around."

"There's still the issue of the diaries," Margaret said.

"What could Hugh Lonsdale possibly have said about anybody that everybody didn't know already?" Donny asked. "Everyone he made headlines with is either dead or dormant.

Or else somebody has already written it up in some tell-all biography. People," he said solemnly, "seem to have no shame nowadays."

"We'll never know until we locate them," Margaret said. "There's something that Bedros doesn't want known, and who knows what else. I say," she said suddenly, "that woman who walked in, the one with the extraordinary hair, looks awfully familiar. . . ."

Donny looked over his shoulder. "She used to be an important star," he whispered, "but she's nothing now. On the other hand, the three men at the far table are about as important as you can get in this town. Two of the most successful producers around and the head of the most profitable studio. I'd like to get into production. In fact, I intend to. I mean, Jon Peters started with hair, and look what kind of fast track he got on."

"Lady Margaret Priam?" A young waiter placed a telephone on the table. "You have a call."

"I've been thinking," Lulu said without preamble. "Since you'll be staying on, you ought to get out of that hotel and stay up here with me. Plenty of room. It's all arranged. You'll be here to watch out for Bedros. He's not in good shape."

"Perhaps for a day or two," Margaret said.

"Just bring your things around after lunch and Millburne will take care of you. I have to go out this afternoon. Oh, and I've got another surprise for you."

"Yes?"

"Well, if I told you, it wouldn't be a surprise."

When Lulu had hung up abruptly, Margaret said, "Apparently I am staying on whether I want to or not. At least I'll have time to track down Charles, whether he wants me to or not."

"How about looking Debby up? She keeps track of Charles still, you know. The realtor she works with is smack in the middle of Beverly Hills, and she's in and out all the time. Mostly out. I think she actually has two car phones. Well, she's making a fortune now, bless her. She has a gift for real estate. She loathed Sylvie for breaking up her marriage, but if you ask me, she lucked out."

"I could speak to Debby," Margaret said.

"And since you'll be around, I'm thinking of having a few people to my place later this week. They'd adore to meet a genuine lady. Half of them have English secretaries, but I think those girls were all milkmaids who managed to brush up on their accents. You know what I mean?"

Remembering Millburne's dutifully acquired upper-class accent, Margaret nodded. "I do, indeed. And what about Cherylle? Will she and Charles marry now, if he doesn't go to jail for murdering his wife?"

"Speaking as a professional advisor," Donny said, "Cherylle needs a *lot* of work. Right now she's a plaything, good for enraging Sylvie, but since Sylvie's gone, what's the point? Look at the time! I do have to run. The life-style business won't wait."

"You advise others?"

"Certainly. I did Sylvie on Wednesdays. My Monday client was kind enough to give me the morning off for my personal business, but I promised I'd be there this afternoon. She's the wife of a studio executive, and you know how important it is to stay on good terms with those people."

"Before you go," Margaret said, "if one were staying at the best hotel, where would one be staying?"

"Beverly Wilshire, here in one of the bungalows, the Bel-Air, L'Ermitage . . ."

"A start," Margaret said. She was determined to track Iris Metcalfe down.

"Look, I'll ring you tomorrow about my little get-together. Do say you'll come."

"Half a promise," Margaret said. "I don't know exactly what lies ahead."

"Well," Donny said, "if you're looking ahead, I'd say staying with Lulu should prove interesting, although it's very restrained compared to the old days. Still, Lulu likes to see people have a good time."

Then Donny was off in a rush, but not so great a rush that he didn't have time to pass by the table with the three men who were as important as one could get and speak a word or two.

Chapter 12

*M*argaret *checked* out of the Beverly Wilshire and into Lulu Lambert's estate.

"Very pleased to have you here," Millburne said. "Madame thought you would be comfortable in one of the guest houses rather than in the main house." He led her to one of the tangerine-colored bungalows, followed by the Mexican boy with her bag. The foliage surrounding the bungalow was thick and the flowers planted along the flagstone path to the door were colorful.

"Millburne, I understand that Mrs. Code was staying here after she separated from Mr. Code."

"That is correct," he said.

"Here in a bungalow or in the main house?"

"She had a favorite suite of rooms in the west wing of the big house," Millburne said.

"And Mr. Kasparian?"

"He is in his room. You can ring him from your telephone. Number seven."

Margaret looked around the sitting room of her bungalow, which was committed to none of the follies she had noted in the main house: white walls, plump red cushions on the sofas and easy chairs, a bold Navajo rug on the floor, and a raised fireplace on one wall. The two bedrooms, one on either side of the sitting room, were somewhat self-indulgent—one was predominantly black and the other mostly gold, and each had a truly enormous bed. There was a tiny kitchen with a refrigerator stocked with snacks and several bottles of champagne. The growing things outside the windows blocked prying eyes. One could live here for weeks on end and never be noticed.

The first thing Margaret did was ring number seven.

"Bedros, I don't know what you are up to, but we need to talk."

"Margaret, I was hoping you'd call. No, no. Don't worry. I am here by permission. When can we meet? I can be driven—"

"I am right here," Margaret said. "Didn't Lulu tell you? I'm in one of the bungalows." Beyond the foliage that half blocked the window she saw a person passing by furtively. "Wait one moment."

She had no clear view from the window, so she opened the door and looked out. Whoever it was had vanished into the dense masses of philodendrons and palms and other rampant growth beyond the bungalow. A gardener or a maid? Perhaps unprovoked attacks by black cars had made her jumpy.

"Bedros, we will meet in half an hour. Outside by the pool. Are there other guests staying here, do you know?"

"One or two, perhaps," he said. "Lulu always has people. I have kept to my room except for the service."

"Has anyone approached you about the diaries?"

"Not exactly," he said. "I'll tell you about it."

"I want to change clothes," Margaret said. Then she realized that she had very little to change into. Dare she take the time to shop? Yes, she decided, if only to enjoy a respite from thoughts of death. "Perhaps we should meet later," she said. "I have some business to attend to. About five?" That gave her a good two hours and more. "Has anyone mentioned seeing Iris Metcalfe?"

"Not to me," Kasparian said, which was not precisely a denial.

Margaret's first business was to ring the luxury hotels that Donny had named. Iris Metcalfe, at least under that name,

was not resident at any of them. Then she telephoned Charles
Code's office and was told that he was in conference and was
not to be disturbed. She was beginning to despair of ever
meeting him.

She set off to buy a few things to wear in the California
sunshine, thinking she ought to have retained Donny Bright
to shorten the process of seeking out the right places to shop.
However, with a bit of money in hand, one could make do
with what was available by stretching out a hand and pluck-
ing something off a rack.

As Margaret sped down toward the flatlands, she realized
that she was mimicking those ladies she had seen on her way
up—off on a shopping spree. It was quite easy to slip into the
local behavioral patterns.

The streets around Rodeo Drive were extraordinarily generous in offering places to park, and they were mostly free.
Margaret, who was accustomed to paying exorbitant rates to
retain a parking space in her New York building, and worse,
the seven dollars or so for half an hour in a Manhattan parking garage, thought that Beverly Hills, in this respect, was a
dream come true.

Rodeo Drive, with its carefully tended, carefully shaped
trees and its glittering shops—very small ones, actually, for
all the world-class fashion names they harbored—was awash
with more tourists than shoppers. Japanese visitors seemed
especially taken with the idea of videotaping the scene.

Margaret was about to be overwhelmed by stunning clothes
and accessories and astonishing prices: Gucci, Valentino,
Fred Hayman, Bottega Veneta, Sonia Rykiel, Ralph Lauren,
Hermès, Ungaro, Saint Laurent, Cartier, Louis Vuitton, Bi-
jan. It went on and on, and there were more shops on the
side streets and the ominous promise of yet more in a mall-
like building a couple of stories high that loomed where Rodeo Drive and Wilshire Boulevard met.

She looked in some windows, examined several unsuitable
garments, then escaped down a side street to walk in the
shade for a block or two. She glanced in more windows that
offered far too many choices for someone with very little
time. On a whim she entered a shop that called itself Majestic

Jewels and found herself admiring a case of artful counterfeit gems that looked like they cost millions.

"I do like emeralds," she said to the young woman who offered her assistance. "I didn't bring mine along."

"Seventy-five dollars a carat," the young woman said, "and nobody knows the difference. Really. They're perfect."

Not many minutes later Margaret departed with a rather splendid four-carat *faux* emerald ring that put her mother's genuine article to shame—plus the suggestion from the salesperson that she head for the department stores on Wilshire to solve her problem of a few things to wear. Of course, Neiman Marcus, Saks, and I. Magnin weren't cheap, but one-stop shopping had its advantages.

Margaret enjoyed her brief respite from the problem of murder. Now she needed to get back to business. She realized that Debby Zahn's office was only two blocks away from where she stood. It was an easy matter to find her way there, pausing at the traffic lights that blinked their commands to walk/don't walk in short spurts while thin, tanned, fashionable women stopped and started in counterpoint to the stops and starts of expensive autos. New York traffic's concentrated aggression vis-à-vis pedestrians had not infected Beverly Hills.

En route to Debby's office, Margaret was perversely pleased to encounter a filthy, bearded man carrying his life in green plastic trash bags: an actual homeless person here in the midst of extraordinary wealth. He shuffled purposefully along the pavement, intent on some goal that only the homeless know. More than even in New York, this reminder of the degrees of wealth and poverty that exist side by side was startling. No one else on the street appeared to be aware of him.

The real estate firm for which Debby Zahn labored was located in a Spanish-style stucco building with a discreet brass sign. Through the large plate-glass window Margaret could see a row of attractive young men and women working the phones at their desks in a room tastefully furnished in shades of gray with touches of deep maroon.

The receptionist glowed with the artful application of paints and powders and carefully induced blondness. She was not sure she could locate Debby Zahn for Lady Margaret. However, after some careful maneuvering of a long, bloodred-tipped finger to press some digits on the maroon phone's keypad, the receptionist spoke Margaret's name. Within milliseconds the sleek woman seated at a desk but two feet away from the reception area walked over to greet Margaret.

"Debby Zahn," she said. "I noticed you at the service this morning." She was young and confident, attractive and well-put-together.

"How . . . nice to meet you," Margaret said. "I'm not altogether certain why I felt I ought to see you, but . . ."

"I imagine Sylvie poured poison into your ear about me," Debby said, "and Charles as well. Reason enough to want to get a look at me, although I like to think of myself as the injured party in the divorce."

"I can say with absolute truth that Sylvie never mentioned your name to me," Margaret said, "and I have only spoken to Charles Code two or three times on the telephone, in regard to Sylvie's burial. I knew your name originally from your former mother-in-law."

"Bea? Quite a nice woman. Come along to the conference room where there aren't so many idle ears to listen to my business."

Debby took the massive, modern chair at the head of the slate-gray conference table. "Bea is always worried about her grandchildren," Debby said, "but I've tried to convince her that they are as all right as can be expected of children with multiple parents and caretakers. Actually, I've only made three mistakes about them. Two were the names Charles talked me into giving them, and the third was letting Charles have custody without an argument. I thought it would be best for them and for me. I couldn't have taken proper care of them and have done so well in the real estate game. In spite of my conflicts with Sylvie, she wasn't a bad stepmother. I do see them every week."

"Will you get them back, now that Sylvie is gone?"

"Charles would fight it. He doesn't readily give up what he has. That tart he's taken up with is pretty awful, but he'll certainly never marry her. Trust me on that. With Sylvie gone and all the money she would have gotten still safely in his hands, he's going to be looking for quality, or what passes for it out here. I would have bet anything that Charles murdered Sylvie, but I don't know how he managed it."

"There are planes," Margaret said. "Anyone could be in and out of New York in a day." Even Debby Zahn, she thought.

"He was back and forth between the coasts like a yo-yo," Debby said, "so he certainly knew his way around the airports. He has some pretty big clients on both coasts, and he is forever trying to get close to the money men in New York who are the real powers behind the studios. He wants to step up from merely lying and cheating and making deals as a lawyer to lying and cheating and making deals as the head of a studio. You know, that's a real high-concept idea: a bicoastal murder. He'll probably get someone to write a treatment to star one of his clients."

"I have never met him," Margaret said. "He is never in. I believe he is avoiding me."

Debby looked at her curiously. "I saw him go into the church ahead of me this morning. He must have gone into that little room near the back and then went to sit with the children by another route. I thought maybe he didn't want to run into Lulu. He's trying to buy her house, you know, and is willing to pay big, big bucks, just for a tear-down. He wants to build something grand. The Lonsdale place is a fright anyhow, and would cost a couple of fortunes to renovate. I've been delicately negotiating with Lulu on his behalf." Then she added, "Even with the divorce pending, and a division of spoils imminent, he never seemed to doubt that he'd have the money to buy when Lulu was ready to sell. That's the kind of brass that works in this town."

The maroon phone at Debby's end of the table rang. "I told them no calls. Yes? Oh, sure. Put her on. Alex, honey, what's the matter? Of course I remembered your birthday. It's just that I'm real busy, so I didn't think to mention it this morning. Yes, I know she promised. I love you, sweetie. You and Dorian do what Fuji tells you." Debby hung up and sighed.

"Apparently Sylvie promised her a big party," Margaret said. "I had occasion to visit Cherylle this morning and spoke to the children."

Debby gave her a long look. "And what did Miss Cherylle have to say?"

"Only that she was away at a spa the day Sylvie was murdered, and she had no idea where Charles might have been."

"She *looooves* going to spas. Plenty of tennis, lots of pampering, exercise, healthy food, green mudpacks, and all that stuff. She thinks it gets her in shape."

Margaret was thoughtful. "I see," she said. "Well, about this party. Do you suppose Sylvie planned to hold it at Lulu's since she was in residence there? Donny Bright didn't mention a thing about it. Perhaps I can find out. I'm staying at Lulu's."

"Are you, indeed," Debby said. She seemed to find the idea amusing. "Well, Lulu's place would be as much fun for kids as it can be for grown-ups. I'd hoped that with the upset about Sylvie moving out and Cherylle moving in, the party had been forgotten."

"Although I am not an expert by any means," Margaret said, "I don't think children forget so easily. If Sylvie's things are still where she left them when she went to New York, I may find that everything is organized and it will merely be a matter of greeting the little guests."

"I'd really be grateful if you could find out," Debby said. "Otherwise I'll have to do something fast. Charles won't, and Cherylle won't. I've got dozens of appointments for the rest of the week. A couple of important houses have just come on the market. Where in hell do these people get their cash, I'd like to know. Everybody can't have looted the national treasury, there can't be that much oil in Saudi, there can't be that much South American drug money. Well, it's not for me to question where it comes from, as long as I get a piece of it." Debby stood up. "Find out about the party, if you can. You can always reach me on my car phone if I'm not here.''

"I'll ring you," Margaret said. "In any case, it can't be too difficult to feed cake and ices to seven-year-olds.''

"You don't know Beverly Hills kids, lady. They expect the works: elephants, clowns, Michael Jackson if you could get him. At least they're too young for high-grade cocaine. That cuts down on the expense.''

"I see," Margaret said. "Rather different than I pictured it. Ah. One more question. When you arrived at that little church this morning, you didn't happen to see a couple— people you know—coming out from that private garden off to the side? Or were you yourself talking to someone there before the service?''

"Not me," Debby said. "I told you I saw Charles come in, but we didn't speak. We don't, unless it has to do with real estate or the kids. Pete Frost was there, too. Neither of them were with any woman. Cherylle had the minimum good taste to stay apart and quiet. I suppose you've heard from people that something was going on between Pete and Sylvie, but that's nonsense. They were simply united in wanting to do Charles in. Winnie Lonsdale came in alone, too. Wow! Look at the time. I've got to show a house in Holmby Hills while the owner is still in Vegas gambling away what he has and hoping that I'll sell for five so he'll have that much more to lose at the blackjack tables.''

"Five?''

"Five million. Awful house, no land to speak of, but a great address. Can you believe it?''

Debby walked with Margaret to the door.

"At least you didn't suggest that I flew east and shot the woman who stole my husband," Debby said.

"You might have," Margaret said, "although I doubt it. Do you truly believe Sylvie stole Charles from you?''

"She was so beautiful," Debby said, "and I merely look really good. Well, okay. He was ready to be stolen. But that doesn't mean I liked the idea.''

Chapter 13

"*I* had to buy a few things to wear," Margaret said to Kasparian. He was waiting for her at poolside at Lulu's, sitting under a massive umbrella out of the afternoon sun. He looked quite unlike himself in a pale lime-green shirt and white Bermuda shorts. Margaret had never seen him dressed in anything but a highly conservative charcoal suit that gave way to a light blue blazer during the hottest New York summer days.

Margaret had quickly changed into a flowered sarong skirt, which continued to be a recreational fashion, and an oversized turquoise T-shirt. Her new counterfeit emerald ring looked quite divine in the sunlight.

She had scarcely seated herself before Millburne was at the table ready to provide their heart's desire.

"I recommend the lemonade," he said, "unless you'd like something stronger."

"Lemonade for the moment," Margaret said. "Millburne, did you hear anything from Mrs. Code about a birthday party for Alexandra?"

Millburne looked slightly pained. "I had hoped that it had been put aside, Lady Margaret. Madame had agreed to have it here on Saturday, and Mrs. Code made some arrangements with a firm called After-Five Fantasies that specializes in parties for children over five years. I do not know the details.''

"Would they be in Mrs. Code's rooms?"

"Perhaps," Millburne said.

"Then I will speak to you later," Margaret said. Millburne departed with dignity to fetch the lemonade. "Possibly, Bedros, I will convince the butler to give me a free run of the house, so I can find information that will help salvage your existence.''

"That would be a comfort," Kasparian said. "I spoke with young Paul Castrocani several times before I left New York. He seemed to feel that he was obliged to keep track of me.''

"He is a good boy," Margaret said.

"Ideally suited to this lavish kind of life.''

"He would love it," Margaret said.

"I do love it," Prince Paul said grandly. "I do." Paul himself had come out of the big house and was standing behind Margaret's chair. He was another who was rarely seen by Margaret in anything but a conservative banker's suit or black tie. In colorful bathing trunks and a handsome expanse of manly chest, he looked as though he had come home. But then, how many years of his young life had been spent in idle, sunny luxury around the world? Beverly Hills was but another stop on that tramline.

"Paul, what *are* you doing here?"

"Dear Margaret, I am Kasparian's keeper. It was De Vere's idea." Paul stretched out his arms and admired the rippling muscles. In spite of being trapped in Manhattan, he did make a point of working out. "I shall acquire a tan here at least.''

"De Vere?"

"He thought I ought to accompany Kasparian for appearance's sake. And he seemed somewhat concerned about you as well," Paul said, but he was looking beyond Margaret at a curvaceous young woman who had emerged from the shelter of the poolside cabana and was adjusting her pink string bikini.

"Concerned, you say?"

"He strongly disapproves of murder," Paul said.

"He might have come himself," Kasparian explained, "but he had the usual pressing police business."

Margaret was oddly comforted by the fact that it might have been De Vere who had materialized at poolside rather than Paul.

"I think De Vere might have found this house somewhat too rich for his taste," Paul commented. "And possibly Mrs. Lambert as well."

"Now that we are here," Margaret said, "shall we discuss this murder? Do sit down, Paul. The young woman will not vanish, and if she does, another will appear. It seems to be the way of this house."

"I am here on serious business," Paul said.

"It seems to me that except for the murder, nothing is especially serious here," Margaret said, and accepted an icy glass from Millburne, who had returned to fawn a bit over Paul.

"Prince Paul, I trust everything is satisfactory. Will there be anything else?"

"For me, nothing," Paul said, very princely. "I am content."

"When will Mrs. Lambert return, Millburne?"

"Not for some time, m'lady," he said. "She is undergoing serious reconstructive processes, although they are not surgical in nature."

When Millburne had retreated to the lair of a butler, Margaret said, "Kasparian, I really do need to know, very simply, the history of Hugh Lonsdale and these diaries that have put you into the middle of a mess."

Kasparian gazed out over the pool where the young woman barely in pink was dangling her toes in the water. "Even though you are both young compared to me," he said, "you must have experienced occasions when people you have met in the past and nearly forgotten return to life, as it were—your life. That was Hugh. Years before the war, before I came to America, I was living in Paris doing a little dealing in pictures, buying and sometimes selling works that are now very well known. Hugh would come across from England; he was someone you met in the cafés and clubs and on the boulevards. He was not yet a successful actor, although he was quite a successful Don Juan. And a daredevil, a devil-may-care. Sly and bold and not altogether trustworthy. Someone—one of the Kordas, perhaps—put him in a popular English film and he went on to Hollywood. There he became a star, although it became evident that his character was unchanged."

"What of Winnie?" Margaret leaned forward to catch every word. Paul stretched out in his chair, eyes half closed, watching the girl and listening to Kasparian.

"I cannot imagine why he married at all—but then I believe she was a spectacular beauty in her prime. When the war came in '39, he left her behind and went back to England to do his duty. I find genuine heroic gestures untypical of Hugh, but trying times bring out some good in some people."

"And what of you?"

Kasparian shrugged. "I was a struggling dealer in this and that in New York. I was not fit for military service, but . . ." Kasparian pursed his lips and seemed reluctant to go on. "With the world seeking ways to come to America and escape the war, I was one who wanted to go back."

"I do not understand," Margaret said.

"I had a way in through neutral countries; I had several passports that were still valid. I knew that there were treasures for the taking—buying—from people desperate to get enough to survive, to escape if possible. I went back to Paris during the German occupation, and there I found Hugh."

"In Paris? In the midst of a war?" Paul had become engrossed in Kasparian's tale, his buxom beauty forgotten. "How could that be?"

Kasparian smiled grimly. "I found him holding court in a neighborhood bistro where we used to meet in the old days. He had changed his appearance some—the mustache he habitually wore was gone, he was unshaven and shabby, speaking like a peasant rather than a famous film star. His command of languages was always exceptional. Naturally I pretended not to know him until we had moments alone. I learned then that he had been sent by the British to engage in liaison work with the French resistance. Perhaps he was effective, but I saw him simply as playing one more role, the heroic, bawdy fighter for freedom, defying the occupying forces and cheating death at every turn.''

''These are the times he wrote about in his diaries?'' Margaret asked. ''I do not believe that people engaged in underground activities are encouraged to put such things in writing. At least as they are taking place.''

''He recorded it all, after . . . after Paris,'' Kasparian said. ''He was there to perform his assigned tasks, but I was there for art, and art alone. My greed was driving me and I was not so concerned about the war. Well, perhaps I found exhilaration in reliving the kind of danger I had outwitted as a boy, as a young man. You are both too young to remember the hardships the war brought. The suffering and the fear.''

''But I know,'' Margaret said. ''Mummy had tales of soldiers billeted at Priam's Priory, to its temporary ruin, and how hard it was to get food. The bombings in London and the children sent off to the countryside to escape. And after the war and into the fifties when I was born . . .''

Kasparian shook his head. ''You are still too young to remember. In 1943 and '44 there were still old friends who had stayed on in Paris who retained treasures from happier days. The old masters, the priceless furniture and sculpture—those the occupying Germans could see and take if they wished. But in the attics and basements there were pieces of canvas worth a fortune, and there were willing sellers.''

Kasparian got up from his chair and walked to the pool, to stare into its deep blue-green depths. The wench on the far side waved, but he did not see her. Then he turned back to Margaret and Paul.

''There was one friend in particular. He had sent his son and daughter to America when the invasion came. His wife had died, and he lived alone in the respectable bourgeois home where he had spent his life. He went about his legal business, bearing the difficulties of the time but not believing that he was in danger. The family had come to Paris some generations before from Alsace, and although somewhere there were Jewish roots, he did not think of himself as a Jew.

The deportation of citizens did not always impinge on the minds of people trying to make their way through difficult times."

The shadows were growing longer as the day began its decline into evening. The bather had been joined by two other young things who were served drinks by Millburne.

"Hidden in my friend's attics were two Renoirs, some works by Matisse, Mary Cassatt, Monet. Beautiful, beautiful. I remembered a Degas, and a Gauguin, only one but superb. The art market was quiet because of the war, but I knew that once it was over . . . My friend and I met and talked after so many years, and I arranged to purchase the paintings, the rolled-up canvases that would feed my greed. We agreed that the money we arranged would be used for the welfare of his children in America until the war ended. But I needed help, I discovered, to take my treasure trove away from Paris. I turned to Hugh and his underground connections. Perhaps I was not as careful as I should have been, perhaps the idea of outwitting the authorities had made me blind to the dangers. Somewhere in the course of my planning, I spoke the wrong word to the wrong person. One night my friend was taken from his house and put on a train that led to a death camp in Poland. I do not even know if the Gestapo knew he had Jewish connections. It was, I think, the perfect excuse to confiscate those artworks I craved."

"But surely no one would blame you now," Paul said. "It was war. Terrible things happened. My father remembers the war—"

Margaret glared at him briefly, and he was silenced.

"I had to flee—empty-handed—to reach England and then America again. Hugh helped, and then he disappeared into the shadows of the resistance, sharing my secret guilt. When he got back to England, he recorded his experiences and included my shameful adventure. It must never be known, and somewhere those diaries will allow that to happen."

"Bedros," Margaret said, "if the choice is between being accused of murdering Sylvie and having a shameful incident in your past made known . . ."

Kasparian shook his head. "I have learned to live with my

guilt, but the man I sent to death was named René Zahn. He was Maurice's father, Charles Code's grandfather. Maurice has been like a son to me. Although there were no paintings, I supported them both as best I could. I do not want Maurice—or Charles—to know that I sent René to his death. You understand.''

"Is that all there is to tell?" Margaret asked. "I still don't see—"

"A little more to tell," Kasparian said. "I have said that Hugh Lonsdale was not trustworthy, that he lived his life as though it were a film role. From what I know about what he wrote down, he dramatized the events to a degree that distorted them considerably. He told me, back before he died. It sounds as though I sent scores of innocents to their deaths, that I myself made a point of informing the Gestapo.''

"I think you can defend yourself," Margaret began.

"There is one last thing," Kasparian said. "Since Sylvie's murder I have had a letter. Unsigned, unidentifiable. It was postmarked Los Angeles. It said that the truth of Hugh Lonsdale's diaries would be revealed.''

"Were you asked to pay for silence?"

"No," Kasparian said, "but it is only a matter of time. That is why I contrived to beg to be allowed to come here for Sylvie's funeral. I had not been charged, I entrusted my passport to De Vere to assure the authorities that I did not plan to flee the country, and since Paul agreed to come with me . . .''

"Do you believe that the person who wrote you will contact you here?"

"Perhaps," Kasparian said.

"What were these diaries like? Large, small?" Paul asked.

"Black leather," Kasparian said. "So big, I believe." He indicated with his hands six or eight inches.

"I had an idea," Margaret said, "even before I knew you were here, that Sylvie had not taken those infernal diaries with her. Could she have left them behind here in this house where she stayed last? I was thinking of doing a search, and now I have the excuse of looking for the plans for the child's birthday party."

"Dio," Paul said with a touch of desperation.

"It will be perfectly simple," Margaret said. "I have an ally in Millburne."

"It seems to me more likely that Sylvie Code would put these valuable diaries in a safe deposit box," Paul said. "People with such objects often do that sort of thing. Even at United National Bank we have such boxes, where people can hide their bearer bonds and jewels and anything else readily converted to cash. I do not believe that anyone would be so stupid as to leave such things lying about."

"Nevertheless," Margaret said, "I will look. Where is Millburne?"

"I will not assist you," Paul said.

"I didn't expect you to," Margaret said. She was momentarily distracted by the sight of Winnie Lonsdale flitting through the shrubbery at the far side of the pool. Winnie was wearing something white and gauzy that floated behind her. Evidently she had put off her formal mourning for Sylvie and slipped into something more comfortable. Winnie hugged a large plastic bag to her bosom as she edged furtively past the cabana at the far side of the pool and now approached the trio of bathing beauties at their shady table. She spoke to them, then continued her progress around the pool until she reached Margaret, Paul, and Kasparian.

Kasparian stood up and bowed slightly. "Will you join us, Winnie? We were reminiscing about the old days."

"I remember the old days," Winnie said. She took a seat and gathered her chiffon scarves about her. "I don't forget much. This house used to be alive, alive with the very best people, classy people. Stars, big stars. Directors, men who ran the studios, producers. Gary Cooper. Remember how handsome he was?" She peered at Margaret. "Do you?"

"Yes, certainly," Margaret said quickly, but Winnie had taken close note of Paul.

"Are you somebody?" she asked. "I've lost track of the new faces. Very good-looking boy you are."

"I am not in the cinema," Paul said, and as usual when he was emphatically the prince, he acquired a noticeable

accent. He was also not averse to flattery, even from a somewhat dotty old lady.

"Errol Flynn. There was one for you. Hugh liked to ca-
rouse. Something about young girls that makes a man lose
his judgment and his mind. Running around after those little
things with their bobbly breasts and their bare little bottoms.
Where's that old fart, Millburne? I need a drink."

At her words, Millburne approached bearing a tray with a
tall glass filled to the brim. He placed it in front of Winnie.

"Hope you didn't louse up the vodka with a lot of tonic,"
Winnie said.

"It is the way you like it, Mrs. Lonsdale," Millburne said.

"Bedros, what are you doing out here creeping around
like a half-dead person?" Winnie asked. "I suppose you
were sweet on Sylvie, too, but it's too bad. She got Hugh and
somebody got her. Bang!" Winnie chuckled.

"Mrs. Lonsdale," Margaret began.

"Lulu doesn't keep this place up at all. I kept it beautiful.
She just has all these little cookies around to amuse the old
guys. At least that's a step up."

"You must have a vast fund of memories," Margaret said.

"Oh, I do. Lady Margaret, is it? Is that a made-up name?
Hugh was English, too. What a man he was, nobody like
him. I stuck with him, right up to his death. We weren't even
speaking the last twenty years, and I stuck."

"I understand he was quite a person," Margaret said,
catching Kasparian's eye.

"Monstrous old devil he was. But I didn't let him get away
with anything. Not me. I stayed on to haunt him to his last
day."

Paul was beginning to look pained, and then more so when
Winnie again turned her attention to him.

"You really are a fine-looking specimen," she said.

"Did I introduce you?" Margaret asked. "Prince Paul
Castrocani, a dear friend."

"Looks a bit young to be your boyfriend, but no harm in
that. I had a couple of boyfriends Hugh never even knew
about. Big stars. That's what I went for. That'll surprise a
few people when they find out."

"Find out?" Margaret asked.

"Yeah," Winnie said. "I'm going to write my memoirs. I've got a publisher back east who's very, very interested. Says he'll pay me a fortune if I do it right. That'll set me even with Hugh and the rest of them. Lulu Lambert with her charity. Thinks she's queen of this place, but it's still mine. She tries to lock me out. Ha!"

"If you will excuse me." Paul stood up. The young women on the other side of the pool were proving more of an attraction than Winnie Lonsdale's rambling reminiscences of Hollywood's distant age of glory.

"I am rather tired," Kasparian said. "I believe I will lie down."

The two men went their separate ways, and still Winnie talked on. "I remember when Gable used to come here, Cary Grant, Joan Crawford. Bette Davis. All of them. They loved this house. What is it now, Millburne?" Winnie had assumed the role of lady of the house in addressing the butler.

"There is a telephone call for Lady Margaret," Millburne said. "If you will follow me."

"I shall return, Mrs. Lonsdale," Margaret said, thinking that she probably would not.

Winnie waved a gracious hand. "Take your time. Maybe you can give me some pointers about these memoirs." She took a bundle of papers from her plastic bag. "Lots of juicy stuff."

Margaret followed Millburne into the house.

"We do have a wireless telephone, Lady Margaret," Millburne said. "I thought you might like to have a respite from Mrs. Lonsdale. It is Mr. Code."

"Oh, really? Thank you."

Millburne pointed her to an old-fashioned white-and-gilt phone that might have appealed to Marie Antoinette.

"Lady Margaret here," she said, not certain whether cool and distant or forgiving noblesse oblige, for his obvious rudeness in avoiding her, would be appropriate.

"I understand you have tried to reach me. I apologize. I have a couple of very big deals I'm working on and it was unavoidable. When can we meet? I suggest breakfast tomorrow.''

''Yes, of course.'' At last, Margaret thought.

''Not Hugo's or the Polo Lounge again—I hope the champagne was adequate, by the way. Too many people I don't want to see. The Bel-Air is a perfectly charming hotel. We'll meet there at eight. Is that too early for you?''

''Eight is fine,'' Margaret said. Then she added, not quite truthfully, ''I want to get back here early so that I can work with Winnie Lonsdale on her memoirs. She's found a publisher.''

''Has she, indeed? I doubt it will come to anything.''

When Margaret hung up, she saw Millburne hovering.

''Do you think I could get a look at Mrs. Code's rooms?'' Margaret asked. ''I want to see if there's anything there about this child's party.''

''Mrs. Lambert has instructed that it be kept locked,'' Millburne said, ''to keep Mrs. Lonsdale out. I should have advised you to do the same at your bungalow. She tends to believe that this is still her home and she knows no limits. There is a key, however, placed on the lintel above the door to the suite. When you reach the top of the stairs, turn left. It is at the end of the hall. The Chinese Suite,'' he added. ''Rather overwhelming, but nothing compared to the Versailles dining room or the Egyptian Suite. That reminds me strongly of premature burial in one of the pyramids.''

''Thank you so much,'' Margaret said. ''Perhaps I shall look later. Will there be people about?''

''Mrs. Lambert will be back but is then going out to dine,'' Millburne said. ''Except for Mr. Kasparian and the prince, everyone else has departed. Of course, one never knows where one may encounter Mrs. Lonsdale.'' He looked glum. ''She has never left. She and Mr. Hugh stayed on after Madame bought the house. I believe that death alone will remove Winifred Lonsdale from the premises.''

Chapter 14

Margaret saw that Winnie Lonsdale was drowsing over a yellow lined legal-sized tablet, with a replenished drink at hand. The memoirs were slowly taking shape, perhaps, but Margaret had other matters to attend to. The sky was a pale blue now, with streaks of pink and mauve clouds, and the tall palms silhouetted against it suggested the perfect postcard to send home.

A maid had unpacked her small suitcase and the parcels of today's purchases. Two bottles of somewhat esoteric mineral water had been placed on a table near a sofa. It seemed to Margaret an excessive frill to import water from Eastern Europe, but no doubt someone fancied it would help get the Eastern bloc economy working again.

She dialed Charles Code's home number, and when a Spanish-accented maid answered, she asked for Cherylle.

"Apparently a birthday party has been planned for Saturday," Margaret said. "I am looking into the details and will let you know."

"That's a load off my shoulders," Cherylle said.

"Some firm called After-Five Fantasies was contacted—"

"Oh, that's great! They are terrific; everybody uses them. I don't have to come since Alex's mother will be going, don't you think? Anyhow, thanks a lot."

"Don't thank me," Margaret said. "Sylvie Code ar-

110

ranged it all before she died. Oh, I meant to ask you," she added, as though as an afterthought, "What is the name of the spa Charles sent you to? I was thinking that as long as I'm here . . ."

"Oh, sure," Cherylle said. "La Costa. It's fabulous. Do you want the number? I've got it right here."

The operator at La Costa Spa in Carlsbad, California, was most helpful. Iris Metcalfe was indeed registered, but so sorry, there was no answer in her room. Yes, she was registered for the week.

"No message," Margaret said. "I'll ring again later."

Although it was getting late, she tried Peter Frost at his law firm's offices.

"I've been wanting to talk to you before you left, Lady Margaret," he said. "Could we have dinner tonight? I could join you at your hotel."

"I'm no longer at the Beverly Wilshire," Margaret said. "I'm staying on a few days and I'm at Lulu Lambert's place."

"Are you? I hope you are up to dealing with Winnie Lonsdale. She's a dreadful old bore. Charles handles some legal business for her, and she talks and talks. As if Hugh had an 'estate' to leave."

"But her memoirs ought to make fascinating reading."

"That! I've never seen her write down a word."

"She is writing them now."

"Then I wonder who will pay her not to write them," Peter said. "Since you're out of the hotel, I suggest a place called Pazzia, on La Cienega. Casual and excellent. Eight-thirty? I'll hang about on the street so you won't miss it."

Margaret put on dark slacks and shirt, the better to search a house. Hadn't she seen a film with a cat burglar so dressed? Life was becoming more and more like the movies every moment. Being practical, she took along a large handbag in case she found something worth removing.

The heat of the day had diminished and the sky was beginning to edge toward darkness as Margaret stepped from her bungalow. A light above the door to her bungalow had come on as dusk had fallen, so the start of the path was visible, but the tangled, lush greenery was in darkness.

Through the leaves she spied a light in another, half-hidden bungalow at the end of a path that veered off from the one where she stood. She was tempted to explore: were the delightful young things staying there, or was Winnie a permanent resident of the bungalow?

Margaret stayed at the edge of the path, mostly in shadow, as she approached. What she had seen was an outside light like the one on her bungalow, but around the edges of the drawn curtains was a line of light from the inside. She stepped off the path and walked carefully across the lawn—except that it was not a lawn of grass but of springy ivy. Margaret edged in behind a thick hedge of some prickly plant until she reached a window that should, if the design was the same as her bungalow, allow her a glimpse into the sitting room. The curtains were so closely drawn that it seemed she would not be able to see the room. Then she found a spot where the bottom of the curtain was slightly awry and managed to peer in. Someone appeared to be lying on the sofa before the fireplace. She could just see the top of a head with dark hair, but whether it was male or female she couldn't determine. An air conditioner hummed nearby, so there was no way of knowing if a conversation was taking place. Then she realized that there were two persons there, apparently wrapped in a horizontal embrace, at the very least. She thought retreat might be the wisest course.

Shaded lights had been turned on around the quiet pool, but Winnie had departed, her now empty glass still on the table. Margaret entered the great hall of the main house and was briefly tempted to explore the first floor with its promise of international fantasies. Instead, she dutifully headed up the stairs past Saint Catherine in her window.

Not a sound was to be heard anywhere. Margaret moved quickly past Lulu's sanctuary and down the long hallway with dark walls and a floor of highly polished wood. She barely glanced at the photos of the great and near great, the living and the dead of Hollywood, that covered the walls.

She tried the knob of the door at the end of the hall and found that Millburne had spoken true. It was locked.

The lintel above the door presented a shelf to hide a key,

but it was too high above her head to be easily reached. Margaret looked about for something suitable to stand on. The only possibility was a low, fragile-looking table upon which stood a bit of dull metal sculpture, an attenuated and possibly female figure. She carefully placed what might be a Brancusi on the floor and moved the table next to the door. She tested her weight on it gingerly and found it was not as fragile as it looked. As she stepped up onto it, she clung to the doorjamb to steady herself in the event that the table did choose to collapse beneath her.

She reached up and felt along the top of the door. Just as her fingers touched the key, she heard voices coming up the stairs. She grasped the key in her hand and froze.

"I don't want to discuss it," Lulu Lambert said, still out of sight but not out of hearing.

Margaret looked for concealment, but there was none. This was a ridiculous position for a lady of her station to find herself in. If she stepped down from the table, she could not easily hide herself in the shadows, although this part of the hall was not well lighted. There seemed absolutely no chance to remain unnoticed. The best solution seemed to be to stay deathly still on top of the table and hope for the best.

She looked down. "Oh, no," she said under her breath. "Shoo." Lulu's little dog was looking up at her, idiotically delighted to discover a playmate.

"I do *not* intend to sell," Lulu said, then she appeared at the top of the stairs, magnificently coiffed with swirls and whirls of piled-up platinum hair. She was followed by a dark-haired man. Margaret squinted, then almost gasped. It was surely Charles Code. The brief sight of him was a revelation. True, his profile reminded her of his father, Maurice, but he was more familiar than that. Margaret was thinking hard, as the two of them disappeared into Lulu's boudoir and the door was firmly closed. The dog scampered down the hall and barked once. The door opened and the dog vanished inside. Margaret breathed a sigh of relief and very quickly stepped down from the table, shoved it aside, and unlocked the door.

It was totally dark in the room. She ran her hands along the wall on either side of the door to find a light switch. She felt something promising and pressed. The place was suddenly illuminated by subdued lamps in several corners of the room. The light was pinkish rather than clear white, and the room and the bedroom beyond through a wide door topped by something like a silhouette of a pagoda was amazing.

Hugh Lonsdale, or whoever had received his instructions regarding decor, had succumbed to an opium dream. It certainly was Chinese in character but rather more so. It was relentlessly red and black, with a profusion of lacquer chests with brass fittings, divans with piles of cushions, embroidered silk hangings, Foo dogs, carpets with intricate designs, and cabinets full of jade and ivory pieces. The walls were covered in red silk; the furniture was massive and ornate. It seemed as though a mad set designer had been unleashed to create a Technicolor version of imperial China without paying close attention to the reference books.

Margaret looked at the embroideries and the statues on display. Although she was by no means an expert, they seemed to be flashy imitations rather than the real things.

Where to begin? she wondered. The sitting room where she stood had few places where the accursed Lonsdale diaries might be concealed or where a dutiful stepmother might have placed details relating to a child's party. She went into the bedroom.

She folded back the doors of the closets that lined one wall. The panels were painted with vaguely erotic scenes of lightly clad ladies with blank white faces cavorting in formal gardens with rotund men in voluminous robes. The decorator had veered away somewhat from the mainland and had incorporated a few traditional Japanese figures in his work. The closets held carefully arranged dresses and suits and some formal wear. Sylvie had not succumbed to the lure of glitz but had opted for understated good taste. Her shoes were arranged on shoe trees in an orderly fashion on the floor. On the shelf above were a few hatboxes, which held, Margaret discovered, nothing but hats.

The doors of a tall black lacquer chest opened to reveal a series of low drawers that held pretty lingerie also neatly arranged. Then, in the drawer of a little writing table, Margaret found a folder marked "Alexandra." A glance through it told Margaret that this had not been planned as a modest ice-cream-and-cake event. Clowns had been booked, a magician, and—horrors!—a monkey. The invitation list was for fifteen children, plus assorted mothers, nannies, and even a father or two. It would all begin on Saturday at two, and beside each child's name was the word "accepted." After-Five Fantasies had already been paid in full—a considerable sum. Margaret wondered whether the price of birthdays escalated as the child grew older and decided that it probably did.

She was a bit put out that Donny Bright had never mentioned a word about Alexandra's party. Surely a life-style advisor advised about such a matter. But very likely even Donny had his limits, and they might not include the lifestyles of the rich and very young.

She took the folder to examine later. Someone at After-Five Fantasies would have to be instructed to take complete charge.

Nowhere in either room was there a place where diaries spanning decades might be stored. The bathroom—black marble, naturally, with gold dragon-headed fixtures—held nothing, although Margaret was quite taken with the idea of a comfortable chaise on which to rest between the exertions of bathing and the long trek back to the bedroom.

The high bed with an ornate black lacquer headboard was covered to the floor with a riotously embroidered red coverlet whereon a dragon and a phoenix were entangled in a stylized dance. Margaret lifted the edge of the coverlet but found that the base of the bed seemed to be a massive block of wood on which the mattress rested. She rapped her knuckles against it and was pleased to hear that it sounded hollow after all. She inspected the base all the way around and found, on the far side closest to the wall, a join in the wood and then, near the floor at the head of the bed, a metal loop flush with the wood. She pulled and the panel opened.

Although the space between the bed and the wall was only a few feet, she managed to pull out one then two black boxes, a foot or so high and three feet long.

In the first were a few bundles of letters addressed to Sylvie and a couple of photo albums. At the bottom of the box were three smaller boxes covered with patterned silk, their covers tied with matching ribbons. Margaret had seen similar boxes often enough. Kasparian's antiques were almost always so packaged. Carefully Margaret untied the ribbon of one box and opened it. Nestled inside in matching silk was a small, pale green jade dragon. This, Margaret suspected, was the genuine article. She opened the other boxes and found a snuffbox in one and a luminous porcelain plate in the other. She replaced the objects and retied the ribbons.

The glass-fronted cabinet in the other room was full of cheap imitations. She had just held three rather valuable examples of the real thing. Could the late Hugh Lonsdale and the present owner of the house be the inadvertent source of Sylvie's supply? Take a genuine piece, substitute a fake, and then on to New York and Kasparian and the money that Iris indicated was so dear to Sylvie. A life-style advisor might assist in selecting the pieces, finding replacements, sharing in the profits. Or why bother to make substitutions here? Hugh wasn't around to complain; Lulu didn't appear to take much interest in the contents of the house. Who would know?

Then Margaret remembered that there was someone who might know and might complain: Winnie. Who might have told Lulu, who might have told Hugh's old friend Kasparian that he was receiving stolen property. Would that bring suspicion of murder around again to him?

Margaret put the silk-covered boxes back where she found them, pushed the black box back under the bed, and pulled out the other one. This looked more promising. It was heavy and filled with leather-bound books, every page covered with careful script. Hugh Lonsdale's diaries at last! Margaret was elated. Kasparian was safe from potential blackmailers. Now she couldn't resist looking quickly at what they had to say. She leafed through two that dated from the mid-thirties, when Hugh Lonsdale had arrived in Hollywood with a fat contract, ready to challenge Ronald Colman, David Niven, and Douglas Fairbanks, Jr. Her eye fell on many a famous name: Gable, Flynn, Tracy, Hepburn, Cagney, and Davis. Selznick,

Goldwyn, Warner. Many names she did not recognize, although the incidents Hugh Lonsdale had recorded seemed to focus on the seamier side of life in the golden west. A surprising number of romantic adventures with stars, starlets, shop girls, studio stenographers, and hapless female passersby were graphically described. Hugh's reputation, on paper at least, sounded considerable.

She looked through the books. Where were the ones that recorded Hugh's war years? Her elation was gradually replaced by concern. They were not here. True, early in 1940 Hugh recorded his determination to return to his native England to fight, as he put it, "the dreaded Nazi devils, with the same boldness and bravery displayed by my Elizabethan ancestors in holding back the Armada." Margaret had a vague recollection of a stirring prewar film seen not long ago on late-night television, when the brave English fought off the Spanish Armada, but she could not remember if Hugh Lonsdale had been a featured player. However, it mattered little, since Hugh always seemed to think of himself in cinematic terms, usually in the starring role. She began to search more frantically through the volumes.

She found diaries from the postwar years, brimming with rage over the travail of reestablishing a film career that had never been absolutely top of the line and now was threatened by younger actors. Winnie was mentioned but not quite as the loving wife who had waited while her man fought: "I have told W. to cease her constant nagging if she wishes to remain my wife. Let her write her own diary without prying into mine." Perhaps Winnie's memoirs had had their genesis in a long-ago domestic squabble.

"Thanks to that fool Bedros, I can at least survive comfortably in this primitive California culture," Hugh had written in the same volume. What an ill-tempered creature Sylvie's besotted old beau was turning out to be.

Margaret carefully placed the books in chronological order. Try as she might, however, she could not will into existence the ones from the actual war years, the ones where Kasparian would be mentioned. They simply were not there.

Disappointed, she picked up the volume that began in 1946 and read:

> I have discovered a fascinating woman. Not fascinating physically to me, although she would suit the less discriminating of my so-called colleagues. Her name is Lulu Lambert, and she is the madam of one of the most appealing brothels I have encountered in many years of frequenting same.

Margaret threw back her head and laughed aloud. Lulu explained. The hints and the style. The girls around the pool. The house seemed too quiet for Lulu to be in business still, but old habits die hard. She slipped the volume into her bag for further reading. The last volume of Hugh's life was there, too, only half filled, and that in a shaky hand. It joined the other in Margaret's bag. She rummaged through the rest of the box's contents. A stiff, rolled-up piece of canvas tied with string had a note taped to it in the handwriting of the old Hugh Lonsdale: "To my lovely Sylvie, to carry you through the years when I am gone—H.''

"Don't think you're going to find anything here," a voice said. Margaret quickly dropped the roll back into the box and turned around. Winnie had eased her way silently into the Chinese Suite and was standing, somewhat unsteadily, in the doorway from the sitting room. "You won't find anything here," she said again, "and what you find will be a lie. Hugh couldn't tell the truth if his life depended on it." She took a step into the bedroom and clung to the door frame. "Hugh kept his popsies in these rooms for months at a time. He thought I didn't know who they were. He said they were his nieces. Ha!''

Margaret managed to shove the second black box mostly under the bed and stood up. "I've been looking for the plans for little Alexandra Code's birthday party," she said. "And now I have found them. Perhaps we should leave.''

"Leave? It's my house. Why should I leave? Hugh sold it out from under me to that . . . that . . .'' Winnie sat down.

"Are you referring to Lulu? It seems to me that she has

been most kind to have you to stay. I suppose you know a great deal about her.''

"A brazen hussy. A wonder she didn't spent her life in jail. Everybody knows about Lulu," Winnie said.

Except me, Margaret thought. She said aloud, "Why don't you tell me about her?"

Winnie frowned as though gathering up her scattered concentration.

"House," she said loudly. "House of ill repute. Famous. I know all about it. Sometimes she had her girls dress up like famous movie stars."

"The land of the exact reproduction," Margaret murmured, and glanced at her new emerald ring to which she had become very attached.

"She made a lot of money and retired. Then she bought this place. Right out from under my feet. She couldn't get it out of her system, though. Money and sex. That's Hollywood. She had pretty little things staying here out in the bungalows, all over my house. One of them killed off Hugh, after carousing around all night. Boom! Dead as they come, right here in this room. Served him right, at his age." Winnie looked sad. "I still miss him, you know."

"Was it Sylvie Code?" Margaret asked cautiously.

"Her. No better than she should be, if you ask me. But I'm not saying. Saving it for my memoirs. I'm writing it all down, right from the beginning. Do you remember Larry Olivier? Now there was a handsome man. I always thought he fancied me, but he had the Leigh woman. . . . Write it *all* down. The truth. Truth could bite Hugh right on his butt and he wouldn't recognize it. I could show you what I've written," Winnie said almost shyly. "Get an expert opinion."

"I am hardly an expert," Margaret said.

"A woman of the world then, with no axe to grind. I have to get them written. Need the money. I've got some money coming to me. Quite a lot, you know."

Margaret didn't know and didn't care to get into the matter. "I'd be most interested in reading your memoirs sometime," Margaret said. "I think we ought to go."

"Now," Winnie said. "They're in my rooms."

"I have an engagement—"

"Won't take long."

So Margaret steered Winnie out into the hall. The house was still very quiet, but she could not be sure that Charles or Lulu would not emerge from Lulu's chambers. "You know this house very well, I am sure," she said.

"Who better? I practically built it. Looked at the plans day after day. Followed the builders around to be sure they did it right."

"Is there any way to the ground floor without passing Lulu's rooms?"

Winnie looked at her vaguely. "Way down? 'Course there is. Right back there in that god-awful bedroom. Door set into the wall, staircase down so Hugh could visit whichever 'niece' happened to be residing."

"Let's go, Winnie." Margaret grasped Winnie's frail arm firmly. "Show me the way."

Millburne did not seem surprised when he looked up from his station in the butler's pantry where he was pouring himself a hefty tot of neat whiskey and discovered Lady Margaret Priam and Winnie Lonsdale appearing through a doorway.

"Good evening, m'lady. I trust everything is satisfactory."

"Thank you, Millburne, yes. Although I fear we must gird ourselves for an extravagant birthday celebration on Saturday."

"As I feared," he said, and tossed off his tumbler of drink. "This position is rather more than I bargained for."

"Is Mrs. Lambert in?"

"She is in her rooms," Millburne said. "You can ring her from the telephone in the hall. Dial one."

Winnie was straying off toward a part of the house Margaret had not ventured into. She turned back and signaled to Margaret impatiently.

"I'll ring her shortly. I am seeing Mrs. Lonsdale to her rooms," Margaret said.

"She cannot be contained," Millburne said. "She walks

the halls day and night like . . . like the Priam's Priory ghosts."

"Ah, you remember them, do you?"

"Those were grand days," he said sadly. "Mrs. Lonsdale is becoming agitated." He sighed. "I usually point her in the right direction and hope for the best."

Chapter 15

*W*innie *Lonsdale* opened another door and tottered down a narrow corridor that ended in a short flight of steps. Beyond the door at the top of the steps was a small cluster of dark rooms that might have once been servants' quarters.

"You see what I have come to?" Winnie asked rhetorically. It was so dark, in fact, that Margaret could make out little but some looming shapes in the corners. There was a musty scent like old perfume that had died long ago.

Winnie turned on a lamp that might have been made from an elephant's foot. It cast enough light so that the shadows were driven back. It appeared that the room was crammed with what could charitably be called memorabilia. Uncharitably, it was a lot of junk in a small space. Every inch of one wall was covered with more of the glossy black-and-white photos signed with insincere sentiments and scrawled signatures that lined the hall upstairs. Perhaps Lulu had retained the true legends of movieland and had kindly allowed Winnie the lesser stars. On another wall were some handsome, old-fashioned movie posters—could that be Hugh Lonsdale as a grinning, bare-chested pirate brandishing a cutlass starring in *The Last of the Corsairs*? There were some pictures pinned up with drawing pins, a jumble of landscapes and flowers, and perhaps in the far corner a painting of the young Winnie

Lonsdale with a halo of fluffy hair and an old-fashioned dress sitting in a garden.

A bookcase was packed, helter-skelter, with leather-bound books, but when Margaret cautiously edged over to read the gold stamping, she found they were bound scripts that charted the history of Hugh Lonsdale's career in films. No diaries visible.

"How about a nice drink?" Winnie asked. She fumbled in a cupboard and produced a half-full bottle of vodka and two delicate wineglasses. "Good old Millburne slips me a bottle from time to time, so I don't have to trouble him when he's watching soap operas in the afternoon."

"I think not," Margaret said. "I'll be going out shortly." Winnie pouted, then filled the wineglasses anyhow.

"A small one, thank you," Margaret said, although straight vodka had never been her beverage of choice. She took the tiniest sip and placed the glass carefully on a shelf that held some type of plaque attesting to Hugh Lonsdale's artistic achievements.

"This is most interesting," Margaret said as Winnie shifted a pile of papers from a chair to the floor to find a place for Margaret to sit. "You wouldn't know where Hugh's diaries are, would you? The ones about what he did in the war."

Winnie shook her head, but Margaret couldn't determine whether she was denying her knowledge of their whereabouts or her refusal to comment.

"None of it was true. He made his life sound like the movies."

"Kasparian said that Hugh worked with the underground during the war," Margaret said. "It sounded most interesting."

Winnie's smile was crafty. "Underground. You bet. But it sounded better on paper. For him. Well, that was his charm. He could make fixing a flat tire sound like he was saving the world." Then she said, "It's not easy to grow old alone."

Margaret felt a pang. She had not been as kind as she should have to poor Winnie.

"People here treat me like a crazy old woman," Winnie said. "I'm not. I'm lonely. What do you think?"

"You're certainly not crazy," Margaret said, although she wasn't entirely sure. "You probably have memories that many people will find fascinating."

"My notes are here somewhere," Winnie said. She began to rummage through the papers piled on a table. "They're rough, very rough, but you'll get the idea. You may not believe this, but I was considered a real looker in the old days."

"I can tell you were," Margaret said. "By your portrait over there."

Winnie looked around distracted. "The portrait? Yes, it does look a little like me, but it's not. Just something I fancied. Ah, here's the stuff." She handed Margaret a large, scruffy envelope. "Give it a read and tell me what you think."

Margaret accepted the envelope. "I'll return it tomorrow," she said.

"Going to make a lot of money," Winnie said. "You'll see. Take care of my old age. Are you alone? You're not hooked up with that old Kasparian, I hope. Too old for you. The boy's too young. Ought to find yourself a nice fellow about your age who'll stick by you. No 'nieces.' "

Margaret thought of De Vere toiling on behalf of law, order, and justice far away in New York. He was a nice fellow certainly, and he was about her age, but he might have "nieces" she knew nothing about.

"I ought to leave now," Margaret said. "I have to dress for my dinner engagement."

"Ah, dinner engagement," Winnie said, imitating Margaret's English accent. "How divine. I, too, have an engagement." She refilled her glass. "An engagement with the past. *How* divine."

Margaret put the envelope into her bag, and let herself out of Winnie's rooms. Winnie did not appear to notice her departure.

* * *

Lulu Lambert was seated at her dressing table before multiple mirrors that reflected a glowing splendor. Her platinum hair had been done up in swags and ringlets, and her dress was a mass of blinding blue and silver sequins.

"I'm going out, and I'm taking Kasparian with me," Lulu said. "The poor old man doesn't know which end is up these days."

"I've been talking to Winnie Lonsdale," Margaret said. "A most interesting woman, although sometimes incoherent. She has told me some fascinating tales."

"She does ramble," Lulu said, and touched up already ample mascara. "But she's got a good memory, that one."

"We can hope that she has an editor with a sure pencil to keep the rambling in line," Margaret said.

"Editor?"

"She is writing her memoirs. She's given them to me to read."

Lulu chuckled. At the sound, the miniscule dog flung itself into space from the bed where it had been resting and landed alertly at Margaret's feet. "Dog seems to like you," Lulu said. "Could you fetch it a bit of Häagen-Dazs from the little freezer? He's crazy about ice cream, especially rum raisin. Use the little dish on the floor over there."

Even as Margaret complied with this unlikely request, she found it hard to believe that she was serving high-priced ice cream to a Beverly Hills dog.

"Winnie has been talking about those memoirs for pretty close to forever," Lulu said. "At least since the day Hugh died."

"How was it, exactly, that Hugh died?"

Lulu met Margaret's eyes in her mirrored reflection. "He was an old man. He ran himself into the ground and he died."

"Winnie seems to have a different version, but no matter. She does claim to have a publisher, and the name she mentioned is genuine enough."

"I shall sue," Lulu said serenely, "if she dares to mention my name. But nothing will come of it, you'll see."

"I forgot to ask her how well she knows Kasparian," Margaret said. "I suppose they're all friends because of Hugh."

"Bedros was out here a couple of times during Hugh's last years. She must have met him then."

"And that's when Bedros managed to introduce Sylvie to Charles Code."

"Sylvie was like a daughter to me. The daughter I never had," Lulu said with a fine touch of sentimentality. "I hope I taught her that she must look out for herself, that beauty is fleeting. It does not last forever."

"She apparently took to heart your advice about looking out for herself. Did she . . . um . . . work for you?"

Lulu heaved herself around on the bench and faced Margaret. "Now what do you mean by that?"

"A simple question," Margaret said. "I know that a number of young women worked for you."

"I retired *years* ago," Lulu said with some dignity. "A few little girls are welcome to stay here when they're down on their luck. Sylvie was one of them."

"And what was she to Hugh?"

"Hugh was very fond of her. She was a beautiful girl. Well, you know that. It was almost touching the way he was sweet on her. He liked to pretend he was a young buck again. His whole life had been pretending. Why stop because his circumstances had changed?"

"Was Iris Metcalfe staying here at the same time as Sylvie? I asked because she mentioned that they had shared digs at one point."

"None of my business who Sylvie took in as her roommate." Lulu turned back to her mirror.

"Have you seen Iris lately?"

"I spoke to her not long ago," Lulu said evasively. "She was passing through Los Angeles on her way to make herself beautiful."

"At La Costa, yes," Margaret said. "It's not far away, I understand, but it's also nearer to the airport in San Diego than Los Angeles is. She was at the funeral, wasn't she?"

Lulu shrugged. "Iris is rich. Iris can do what she wants. I have a sense that what she wants just now is Charles Code, but if I came right out and said it, that would be wicked gossip. Are you going to be able to entertain yourself tonight? That good-looking prince found himself a date. I do like to see young people having a good time.''

''One of the girls at the pool?''

''They drop in when they're out of work, or when they aren't seeing some producer or casting person. They all want to be stars. They swim and sit in the sun, have some time to relax, and think about what life has in store for them. I'd hate to be the one who tells 'em. Sometimes they meet one or another of my old pals who like to visit. No harm in that.''

''No harm,'' Margaret repeated, but remembered that Sylvie had swum and sat in the sun, and what life had in store for her was an early death.

''Kasparian, are you in?'' Margaret knew he must be in his room when she knocked. ''It's Margaret.''

The Kasparian who opened the door to her looked as though years had been washed away. Confession, perhaps, had done him good.

''I'm not sure if my news is good or bad,'' she said. ''I found most of Hugh's diaries, but none from the war years. And, tell me, did he know anything about those pictures you were scheming to get from your old friend René before he was taken away?''

''Only what I let slip—he had to know I wanted to get some valuable things out of occupied France.''

''I see,'' Margaret said. ''And could any of the Oriental bits that Sylvie brought you have been taken from this house?''

''Stolen, you mean? I don't know that Hugh had any good pieces, but . . .'' He hesitated. ''I have a few small suspicions, but you know what the antiques business is. You can't check everything.''

''Oh, Bedros.'' Margaret sighed. ''Nothing to be done about it now. I suppose you've had dealings over the years with Winnie.''

"Very little. She never cared much for me. Hugh probably told her tales. . . ."

"She's seriously telling her side now," Margaret said. "I have the start of her memoirs to read. Don't stay out too late with Lulu. Now there's one with a tale or two to tell."

"You've found out about her, then. Well, Margaret, we all have to make our way somehow, preferably in a money-making profession."

Chapter 16

On her way back to her bungalow to dress for dinner with Peter Frost, Margaret noticed that the other bungalow was now dark but for the light over the door. The amorous couple had departed into the deepening night.

She had neglected to lock her door as Millburne had advised her to, but nothing seemed to have been disturbed. Winnie had been engaged in creeping up on Margaret in the Chinese Suite, rather than in inspecting the price tags on her new frocks.

She took from her bag the volumes of Hugh's diaries she had brought with her. She thought she ought to conceal them and Winnie's envelope of memoirs. There were too many people roaming around Lulu's estate. She decided that the folder of party plans could stay right here for all to see. The books and the envelope would go under the mattress in the other bedroom, the black one that was too grim to sleep in, although it might have an appeal to certain tastes.

I. Magnin had kindly provided a short, sexy green dress costing rather more than Margaret usually spent. Somehow, it had looked like Hollywood glamour without going overboard. She knew it would blend well into the background as much as possible. Besides, she thought she looked smashing in it.

She was glad the gates were open at the foot of the drive

as she departed for dinner. She didn't care to find the signal that would open them, thus perhaps taking Millburne away from his evening's rest.

The city at night was quite different from the city by day. At Santa Monica Boulevard a stream of cars stretched in both directions. The neon on the low buildings blinked and glowed and promised hidden delights behind nondescript facades. Margaret had memorized carefully the route to the restaurant and proceeded decorously in what she hoped was the right direction. She still had the grand rental car, but it seemed shoddy in comparison to those which drew up beside her at the traffic lights. Once she looked to her left and found herself locking eyes with a breathtakingly handsome young man in a low, low red car. He smiled at her winningly, seductively, and she smiled back in spite of herself. Perhaps if she had lifted a finger, pointed to the cocktail lounge on the next corner, she would have found herself in a dark room with a candle on the table between them saying, "Are you somebody . . . ?" Or perhaps, "I'm somebody. . . ."

Perhaps he was a beautiful gay man who liked to practice his look on reasonably attractive blond ladies in rented cars, or perhaps he was an aspiring actor who had spent everything on that glamorous car in the hopes of attracting the attention of the wife of someone in the business who could help him. Or . . .

The light turned to green and the red car leaped ahead of her and disappeared into the traffic. When next she stopped at a traffic light the person in the vehicle beside her was a stony-faced Mexican in a pickup truck who looked as though he would endure the hell of this street of dreams as bravely as possible. At the last light before she turned onto La Cienega, the Land Rover at her side was packed with a rowdy, good-natured crew of gloriously blond teenagers, the boys exuding ill-focused virility, the girls bubbling over with giggling, carefree sensuality. The comparatively ancient Margaret held no interest for them. They left her in their dust.

She continued along La Cienega slowly, trying to determine the location of the restaurant. This was a dark street with shops now closed for the night and only a few neon signs to indicate after-dark places of refreshment. She braked suddenly at the sight of Peter Frost on the pavement in front of a building set back from the street. A parking attendant relieved her of her car, then she met Peter at a ramp beside which a sort of stream flowed between concrete banks.

"Hello, lovely to see you again," she said. She looked toward the glass wall of the restaurant. On one side was an uncluttered bar; in the center were café tables with a couple of patrons; and at the other side was the stark, high-ceilinged dining room painted a dark and cream beige, where the tables and well-designed black chairs were already mostly occupied and handsome, dark-haired waiters circulated. "Rather impressive," she commented.

"Very popular and very good," Peter said. "You look very good, too."

Ah, Margaret thought, flattery, and to what end? She said, "Is this considered—what do they say?—a trendy neighborhood?" It seemed to her an unprepossessing street to harbor a popular restaurant.

Peter took her arm and guided her up toward the restaurant. "There are three white stretch limos parked on this side of the street alone. What do you think?"

"I see," Margaret said. "Trendy to the max." The words did not have an easy time falling trippingly from her tongue, but she had always made it a practice to try to speak the language of the natives in whatever exotic locale she found herself.

The greeting at the door was effusive, the waiters highly attentive, the wine excellent, and the food as it was presented quite the best she'd eaten in her short time in California. There was even an opening into the kitchen where one could observe the chefs at work.

"I come here often," Peter said. "If you like it, we can come again."

"I don't know that I will be here much longer. Well, through Saturday unless I can find someone to take over handling Alexandra Code's birthday party."

"Surely Debby could do that. She's her mother. Not that I'm encouraging you to leave." Peter was being very charming. "But then Sylvie was quite devoted to her stepchildren, while Debby has rather shrugged off her responsibilities."

"I think that is perhaps the only true thing anybody has said about Sylvie," Margaret said. "A good stepmother. Everything else one person says about her is contradicted by another. Someone repeats a rumor, and someone else denies it. The relationship between you and her, for example. A romance according to one. Business according to you."

"I told you in New York that it was business," Peter said. "You know, Margaret, you are an attractive woman who should be looking out for yourself rather than messing about in the death of a woman who was nothing to you."

"A great beauty, a greedy divorcing wife, a loving stepmother, a homewrecker, the girlfriend of an old and somewhat bad-tempered movie star. To Winnie Lonsdale, she was no better than she should be. To Kasparian, a courier of precious objects from coast to coast. To another, an alleged blackmailer. A woman who needed a life-style advisor to arrange her life. Perhaps at one time even a girl employed by a now retired but well-known madam."

"That is definitely not true," Peter said.

"And," Margaret continued, "I suggest the possessor of secrets of which I know nothing. Plus the potential of allowing the controlling interest in a successful law firm to be put in your hands."

"I didn't kill her!"

"No, no, probably not," Margaret said, but she was staring up at the high ceiling, thinking.

"Not probably. I did not. Margaret, are you there?" Peter leaned forward.

Margaret smiled at him. "Yes. Yes, indeed. I've just had a marvelous revelation. Sylvie Code didn't die because she was many things to many people, but because she was many things to one person, and all of them were dangerous."

"I don't understand," Peter said.

"But I do," Margaret said, "and I think I know who it might be. But I'll have to get some answers tomorrow." She changed the subject. "The *gelati* are simply delicious." She had been served scoops of rich, dark chocolate, tangy tangerine, and creamy espresso.

"If you're up for it," Peter said, "after dinner we can stop by at a party. A friend is celebrating his anniversary with a kind of open house. It won't keep you up late, though. We go to bed early here. His house is up in the hills, and the view is terrific."

"It's nice to know that people do stay married," Margaret said.

Peter laughed. "It's not a wedding anniversary. He's celebrating the fact that he's held his job at one of the studios for two years. I think that's more important than his marriage, which has lasted several more. You can leave your car here and drive there with me. I'll be sure you get back to Lulu's and she can have one of her boys pick up your car in the morning."

"I'm rather tired," Margaret said. "But why not? I ought to experience all that this strange land has to offer."

"We don't stay out till all hours here," Peter said, "since we tend to start business early."

The parking valet brought Peter's car around to the front of the restaurant. It was low and black, and it had tinted windows. Had it been Peter who had gone off after the service that morning and attempted to demolish the four innocents in front of the Wee Kirk o' the Heather? Margaret had sudden second thoughts about driving off into the night with Peter Frost, in spite of her revelation.

"I wonder if I oughtn't just go on back to Lulu's," she said.

"I know it looks like a lethal weapon," Peter said, "but I was practically born on a Los Angeles freeway." He grinned reassuringly. Margaret was beginning to think he was actually quite a good-looking man and not nearly as fierce as he had seemed in New York. Still, some murderers she had known had been entirely charming.

"This is your car, then?" she asked.

"Not exactly. It's leased by our firm. We all use it when necessary. I have a fabulous Porsche that suffers from frequent unexplained emotional breakdowns and thus spends a lot of time being coddled by men in white coveralls who speak its language. I had to send it in today, so I borrowed this one for the evening.''

"Fancy that," Margaret said. "Psychiatrists for autos. California is certainly an amazing place.''

But who had been driving the car this morning at the cemetery? Once again the answer came around to Charles Code.

Chapter 17

They drove through the darkness up into the hills above Hollywood and Los Angeles.

"Look back," Peter said, "when we round the next curve."

Margaret looked. Spread out at the foot of the hills, stretching out until it touched the dark Pacific Ocean, was a carpet of lights. They glowed, they twinkled, they were many thousand points of light that promised much and probably delivered rather less.

"It's beautiful," Margaret said. "There is much to be said for life in this part of the world." Then the view disappeared as they climbed farther upward on the narrow road that wound its way between hills packed with houses clinging tenaciously to the fragile dirt that showed in bare patches from time to time in the headlights.

Margaret said, "I told you that Winnie Lonsdale is writing her memoirs. What do you know of her?"

"We have met," he said. "I suppose she must remember a lot about the old days in Hollywood, but I have a number of clients who have proposed putting their memories down on paper without much success. On the other hand, she could probably tell some juicy tales about Lulu. You could make Lulu's life into a mini-series, if you ask me, although television isn't exactly ready for the real thing. She was a bawdy old dame who figured out that if you give people what they want, they'll beat a path to your door and pay handsomely. Of course, that was years ago, and by the time I met her she was merely a living legend who'd made so much money she could afford to do what she wanted, whenever and wherever she wanted.''

"Money is good that way," Margaret said. "She never kept up the business in later years?"

"I wouldn't say that," Peter said. "And if so, quite informally."

"And not Sylvie, you say."

"Look," Peter said. "Whatever Sylvie did with her life, it wasn't on a professional basis. I told you that sex was the most popular sport in town. All right, she was close to old Hugh Lonsdale in his last years. I have no idea what was between them."

"Enough so that death did not finally part them," Margaret said. "She's buried next to him at Forest Lawn."

"No kidding? She once mentioned that Hugh was generous."

"Perhaps," Margaret said slowly, "exceedingly generous. How well do you know Iris Metcalfe?"

"I know the name," he replied. "Charles or Sylvie must have mentioned her. Why do you ask?"

"I talked to her in New York before I came out, but I now suspect that there are things she didn't tell me. Someone said he saw her here today. I wish I could locate her, but she's probably at this place called La Costa."

"It's only a couple of hours away," Peter said. "Not a difficult drive, and you'd like it. Gracious and relaxing. Tennis and golf and special spa treatments."

"It's a thought," Margaret said, but did not tell Peter that she had tried to telephone Iris and had been unsuccessful.

They reached the very top of the particular hill they had been climbing. The street was lined with cars parked close to the edge of the road, which itself seemed destined to collapse and send them all tumbling down the hill into the swimming pools below. The house had a tiny driveway where parking boys took charge and drove the arriving cars off into secret spots and neighbors' driveways.

"I hope you are prepared for a unique experience," Peter said. "Marvin Smith is a man who knows how to throw a party. His wife tends to retreat to her room and allow whatever happens to happen."

They entered the house, which seemed to be cantilevered out into space. Then Margaret saw that this entrance building was comparatively small and the house proper descended downward on the side of the hill.

"It is architecturally quite amusing," Peter said. "Hello, nice to see you." This might have been addressed to a departing middle-aged man bookended by two gorgeous women, or he might have been speaking to a group of fleshy, important-looking cigar smokers gathered on a balcony beside the stairs she and Peter had started down. At the foot of the staircase was a glaringly white room with rather preposterous modernistic lighting fixtures hanging from the sixteen-foot ceiling. A few white and black sofas were placed against the walls for the weary about to take the stairs up.

"I don't believe I am correctly dressed for the occasion," Margaret said. She was observing a small but voluptuous woman in a short chiffon dress covered with gold bugle beads.

"You look fine," Peter said. "In fact, you look delectable, and I may be falling in love with you."

"Unlikely," Margaret said, "although I have never been one to deny the magic of specific moments. Should I ask you if you are married?"

"Not presently. Married, that is," Peter said. "Shall we find the party? I think it will be one level down."

The second set of stairs were reminiscent of the steps of a Mayan temple where young virgins were led to their untimely demise. In any case, it was white marble with glass risers, behind which colored lights glowed so that one stepped on translucent blocks of pink, green, and yellow. The niches in the walls were filled with rather decadent representations of nymphs and satyrs.

At the bottom of the stairs, several waiters were gathering

their resources to plunge with loaded trays into the big room, where the party seemed to be concentrated.

"They don't seem to have dressed much," Margaret said. The waiters, in fact, wore purple satin shorts and little else.

"Marvin likes to please every taste," Peter said. One of the waiters looked Peter up and down and winked. Margaret thought that Peter might have winked back, but his hand was caressing Margaret's back in an entirely forthright manner.

The room was filled with exceedingly attractive women on the one hand and exceedingly confident men on the other.

"I see a number of my clients," Peter said. "Hello, darling. You look fabulous. This is Lady Margaret Priam, visiting from England."

The young woman in question appeared not to own a comb, as her blond hair cascaded in uncontrolled kinks and ringlets over her shoulders. She was almost wearing a tiny black satin dress with spaghetti straps that might have been a slip. She did not seem entirely able to focus on Margaret, but she made a brave attempt to be cordial.

"A lady, huh? You look kinda old for Peter."

Peter said, "My tastes are comprehensive. Run along and have fun, that's a good girl. Lots of important producers and directors and casting people who can help advance your career. Trust me, I'm your lawyer."

The young woman thought about it for a second, then swayed off into the crowd on truly impossibly high heels.

"Is she someone I ought to know?" Margaret asked.

"Maybe someday. I took her on as a favor to her agent," Peter said. "She is often in need of the services of a fatherly and understanding lawyer. I believe her career in show business may come to something, although she is presently in the grip of a rather expensive and debilitating attachment to cocaine. We are working on it."

Most of the people were gathered near a white piano listening to two people who were singing very well, indeed, but were definitely not hired for the occasion. Even Margaret, who did not closely follow the American entertainment business, recognized them as near legends, who had decided to sing for their friends at Marvin Smith's anniversary party.

"Goodness!" Margaret said.

"They're great, just great, aren't they?" Peter whispered.

"What? Oh, yes, certainly. But that's Paul. Whatever is he doing here?"

"Paul?"

"Prince Paul Castrocani, a friend from New York who's also staying at Lulu's place," Margaret said. "And where did he find those girls?" That question was entirely rhetorical, since Paul attracted young women effortlessly and sometimes to his dismay. On this occasion he was thigh-deep in adoring wenches. Margaret left Peter listening to the music and joined Paul.

"Margaret sweetheart, what's happening?" Paul had not only picked up a coterie of admirers but the jargon as well.

The girls surrounding Paul looked Margaret up and down, then decided that she was probably not a threat to them.

"I came with a friend," she said. "How do you happen to be here?"

Paul gestured with both hands, the Italian side of him wordlessly expressing the amazing workings of fate.

"It just happened?" Margaret said in an attempt to interpret the gesture. "Someone, possibly previously unknown, invited you on the spur of the moment?"

"Exactly," Paul said. "And there's more." He shook off the girls like a half-grown puppy shaking off the effects of a sudden downpour. "My life has been changed forever. I shall be rich and famous. I shall be able to restore the Castrocani villa, which is decaying faster than the city of Rome itself. I shall retrieve the beloved Ferrari that my mother took back when she discovered how expensive it is to hire round-the-clock protection in New York."

"Do stop and explain yourself," Margaret said. She cast a wary glance at the covey of girls who had withdrawn in a group to await Margaret's departure before returning to their prey.

"I have been discovered," Paul said grandly. "I am to become a film star."

"But you are not an actor," Margaret said.

"Apparently that is not a great problem," Paul said. "After all, I am not a banker, yet I work as one."

"By whom have you been discovered?"

"I have his card. It is a man I encountered here only minutes ago who said that I have star quality. We are to . . . to take a meeting tomorrow."

"Congratulations," Margaret said. She was privately doubtful about the outcome of this adventure, but Paul seemed elated. "I am sure it will delight your mother. And certainly your stepfather."

"Ben Hoopes will be pleased not to have to worry about my financial affairs any further. Ah!" Paul slapped his forehead. "I knew there was something I was to tell you in the morning, but I will tell you now. I was introduced to Charles Code tonight."

"He's here?" Margaret looked around before she realized that she had no idea who she was looking for.

"He was leaving as I arrived," Paul said. "Naturally I did not indicate in any way that I know you and Kasparian."

"Naturally not. Was he alone?" Margaret was briefly distracted by the appearance at Paul's side of one of his girls, who had boldly decided that enough was enough. She put her arm through his in a possessive manner.

"I understood that his lady friend was waiting for him in his car. I did not see her."

"Damn. Well, tomorrow is soon enough. Come over and meet my escort, Peter Frost. Only a marginally potential murderer, who turns out to be quite nice."

"As nice as De Vere?" Paul asked sternly. For a young man who enjoyed the company of many women, he was quite conservative when it came to Margaret.

"De Vere is in a class by himself," Margaret said noncommittally. "Peter, this is Prince Paul Castrocani." Peter was in conversation with a lean man with bronzed skin and a hawklike profile. He was dressed all in white and looked exceedingly well cared for.

"A pleasure," Peter said. "And I, in turn, introduce you to our host."

"How do you do, Mr. Smith? Lovely party."

"Good enough," he said. "Oh-oh. I see that my wife has decided to join us. I better attend to her so that she doesn't store up a pile of complaints to throw at me. Who let that guy in?"

Margaret saw Donny Bright heading toward the woman who was presumably Mrs. Smith.

"It's Donny Bright, the life-style advisor," Margaret said. "He's a pleasant enough chap."

"Bright? Is he the guy who moved in down the hill a couple months ago?"

Margaret shrugged but believed that Donny was angling for a client to replace the dead Sylvie Code on Wednesdays. Donny caught sight of Margaret and blew her a kiss, but chose to concentrate his attention on Mrs. Smith.

While Marv went off to deal with his wife and Donny, who would probably cost him a good deal of money eventually, Margaret said, "Peter, Paul has been told by someone he met here that he is about to become a film star. Is that possible?"

"Margaret," Paul said a bit desperately, "do not destroy my illusions before I have had a chance to enjoy them."

"Who is this someone?" Peter asked.

"His name is Roach. Quintus Roach," Paul said.

"Ah, yes," Peter said. "I advise you not to make a heavy investment on the basis of future expectations. Sorry. Once in a while Quintus and his cousin manage to get backing for some film or other, but it's more talk than action. Now there's something you don't see at every party."

A naked and possibly inebriated man made his way slowly across the room. A few people turned to observe him, then went back to their party conversations. The man proceeded through broad-open doors beyond which an illuminated pool was visible. He sat down on the edge and dangled his legs in the water, then slipped in. The last sight of him was his dark head moving through the blue water to the opposite side of the pool.

"Starkers," Margaret said. "Imagine that."

"About Mr. Roach," Paul said. He seemed downcast as the promise of a glorious future evaporated.

"He makes a lot of sensational discoveries. Puts a lot of ads in the trades. Don't feel too bad, Prince. There are better businesses to be in." Paul looked as though he was wondering whether he could reassemble his fan club now that major stardom was more or less a pipe dream. Margaret was pleased to see that the girls welcomed him back with open arms.

"There are a couple of people I ought to speak to," Peter said. "Business. May I leave you for a time?"

"Please do," Margaret said. "I'll mingle a bit. I keep seeing faces that I know must be famous. I'll just look at them."

Since the naked man had vanished, Margaret headed toward the pool. Donny broke away from Mrs. Smith to intercept her briefly. "Can't stop," he said. "New client, don't I hope. I crashed the party since I live *just* a stone's throw away. Have you discovered the murderer? It could have been Charles. I found out definitely from that secretary that he was out of town. Is he the murderer?"

"Possibly, but I think I have a better idea," Margaret said.

"You have? Fabulous. Who is it?"

"No proof," she said. "I have to figure some things out. I'll let you know."

"Got to get back to my big fish," Donny said. "What a treat, seeing you here."

Margaret took a tulip glass full of what she hoped was champagne from a passing waiter and went out to the pool. The edifice that probably housed changing rooms and cosy corners for dalliance had been made to look like a Greek temple, complete with mostly naked caryatids supporting the roof. She sat down beside the still waters and looked out over the sparkling city.

She thought about Sylvie Code's murderer. Charles Code had eluded her once again, the critical years of Hugh Lonsdale's diaries were missing, and there was something else that troubled her. Sylvie's black boxes hidden under the Chinese bed, Winnie's room full of memories.

"Well, well, all alone? A pretty lady like you?"

Margaret looked up and was relieved to see that it was not

the naked man. "I have been admiring the view. It is one of the finest achievements of mankind."

"Los Angeles? You got to be kidding."

"The distant view of electric light. At close range, a collection of esthetically deficient globes of light. From here, it is nearly art."

"Are you some kind of thinker?" the man asked. "Or a writer? That's it. You got to be a writer."

"No. I am Lady Margaret Priam from New York. I am here tonight with a friend."

"So you're not in the business?"

"If you are referring to the film business, no. Are you?"

"Yeah. Who'd you come with?"

"Peter Frost."

"Oh, sure, the lawyer. His partner was here earlier, Charles Code. Good thing he left before Peter came. They don't get along."

"Do you know who Charles was with?"

"Never saw her before. Classy-looking woman, but not my taste. Too thin. I hear Code's wife got bumped off."

"I was the second person to see the body," Margaret said. "Quite terrible."

"No kidding? You selling the story rights? I could talk to Frost. Is he gonna handle the deal?"

Margaret was amused. "The story of coming upon a dead person? What would the rights be worth?" Obviously one made deals now and worried about the fine points later.

"If we could manipulate the press a little, build it up," he said. "I see it as a big picture, major stars. Play up the revenge angle. Or maybe the guilty secret. *Silenced by Death*—now there's a title."

"No one has actually been accused," Margaret said. "We don't know why Sylvie Code was murdered." But she was beginning to think she did know, and she wanted to get back to Lulu's to look into her suspicions.

The man waved away her objections. "No problem. A beautiful woman like that? Sylvie was one gorgeous dame. Dressed like a queen. Lots of money behind her. I know class when I see it."

"I have to go now," she said, "but this has been delightful."

"What about the story rights? And I see maybe Candy Bergen or Jackie Bisset doing you."

"Ah, yes. Well, I'll have to think about it."

"Here, take my card," the man said. "Have your people call my people."

As Margaret walked back into the house to find Peter Frost, she noted that she had just been discussing a major motion picture with Quintus Roach. Perhaps she should have asked if she could play herself.

She found Peter. "I don't know how long you had planned to stay, but I really ought to leave."

Peter gave her a look that almost said "Your place or mine," followed by one that said "Forget I said that."

"I'll drive you back to Lulu's," he said.

"I'm exhausted, and I want to be at my best tomorrow for Charles. Before that I have a couple of things to do."

"You're quite refreshing," Peter said, as the car sped downhill at what seemed to Margaret like unsafe speeds.

"In what respect?"

"You seem to have your own agenda," he said. "Here I am, a powerful Hollywood lawyer who can make deals Charles Code couldn't match if he lived to be a hundred. I know everybody who matters in this town, but none of that seems to influence you."

"That is true," Margaret said. "You likely do know everyone who matters here, but do you know the Prince of Wales?"

"No. Do you?"

"Not well," Margaret said. "But naturally I know his parents."

Chapter 18

While the various inhabitants of Lulu Lambert's house in Beverly Hills made their way along the highways and byways of Los Angeles, Winnie Lonsdale emerged from her room and crept down the narrow passageway until she reached a door that led into the lofty, *faux* medieval great hall. She had chosen to wear blue tonight. Blue was her lucky color.

Usually she enjoyed the quiet night hours when she could gather to her the memories of the old days when the most famous faces in the world—other than Stalin, Roosevelt, and Churchill—had beaten a path to the Lonsdale door.

Tonight Winnie was uneasy. She might have been saying too much about her memoirs. She didn't trust Lulu not to seek them out and tear them to bits. Nice Lady Margaret had them for the moment, so they were safe. The memoirs would give her back something of what she'd lost in status, but the plastic shopping bag she hugged to her chest was going to bring her much more.

The suits of armor stood guard in the shadows. Faint night-burning lights from the radiating hallways only illuminated the edges of the hall. Winnie peered about furtively to be sure that no one, especially not Millburne, was about. All of the maids but one went off each evening to their families in parts of the city that the residents of Beverly Hills seldom saw. Millburne habitually hid himself away in his comfortable quarters behind the kitchen, to watch the very large television set that kept him company through the long, quiet evenings. In her day there were parties every night, and the butler worked for his money.

She had heard a car earlier, but it had not been followed by the sound of someone entering, so she imagined the last maid or the cook had been driven off by a husband. But that had been the start of her uneasiness.

Winnie looked out the window beside the front door. A row of lights edged the drive. The several cars parked there were dark. She froze at a faint scuffling sound. Mice maybe, or even a rat.

She left the house through a side door that led out to the pool area. The lights there had been shut off except for one at either end of the pool, but she would know her way even if she were blind. There was a faint light on in Lulu's rooms overlooking the pool. She squinted. Was it her imagination or did she see a shadow moving behind the curtains?

Imagination. She had not heard Lulu and that old fool Kasparian return. Winnie stopped and listened again. No sound but the hum of the pool filter. She slipped silently behind the cabanas and made her way along a gardener's path to the bungalows. The locks had been changed on the front doors of the bungalows some time ago, but Winnie alone remembered that they had low doors in the back overgrown with bushes that the gardeners never bothered to prune. The doors brought one into the tiny and entirely unused kitchens that looked like mere closets. She let herself into the bungalow down the path from the one where Margaret was staying and moved very quietly toward the sitting room.

For a second she hesitated, hidden behind the door. The memory of an expensive scent hovered at the edges of the room. Winnie listened but heard no sound to indicate that anyone else was there. She frowned. There was something wrong. The appointment had been very definite.

Winnie stepped cautiously into the room.

The heavy, full bottle of champagne, still icy from the little refrigerator in the kitchenette, struck her on the side of the head. She fell backward, still clutching her plastic shopping bag. She was unconscious as she was half carried, half pulled from the bungalow and dumped into the thick ivy that covered the ground off the path away from the building. A second, more deadly blow was struck. The plastic bag was pried from her hand, and Winnie Lonsdale sank into a green ivy sea.

Not long after, Millburne looked up from his television set and cocked his head. He thought he had heard a car engine, and he waited to be summoned by Madame for anything she might require. But there was no summons. Millburne went out to the front of the house. The Rolls was not parked in its usual place. Madame was still out.

Millburne went back to nod over the telly.

The gates of Lulu's estate were still ajar when Peter drove up with Margaret.

"So glad not to have to trouble Millburne to let me in," she said, "but is it wise to leave one's expensive house open to all who pass?"

"Even we extravagant Beverly Hills folk get careless," Peter said. "Or lazy."

"I say, I'm sorry, too, that I had to trouble you to bring me back."

"I repeat," Peter said, "no trouble. Shall we meet again before you go back to New York?"

"That would be nice, although I have a few things that will keep me occupied for the next day or two."

"Pursuing a murderer or a career in the movies?" Peter had quite enjoyed her tale of the indefatigable Quintus Roach.

"One of those is likely, the other is not," Margaret said. "I haven't decided."

"Then I'll call you soon to see which you have chosen." Peter's car glided off almost soundlessly into the night.

Since Margaret had locked the door of the Chinese Suite from the inside and had retained the key when she and Win-

nie had taken the back stairs, she knew she could get into
Sylvie's old rooms again. What she didn't know was whether
she could contrive to get into the house unnoticed. The front
door would be locked, and she was afraid that even an attempt to open it would set off an alarm. And once in the
house, would she be able to reach her goal undetected by
Lulu in her lair at the top of the stairs?

She went around the house to the pool. It was quiet and
restful. Margaret thought it a pity that New York was so
vertical that the luxury of a pool beside one's home was
reserved for those Arab sheiks and builders of shopping malls
who had had the foresight to acquire several floors of an
apartment building and have a pool built.

Margaret reached out to touch the door, apprehensive
about alarms and worse. She took seriously the threat of
armed response to intrusion. But the door, like the gate at
the road, was ajar.

When she walked through the darkened house, it seemed
to her that she was walking with ghosts who had frolicked
with the young Hugh Lonsdale and, indeed, the young Winnie. She tiptoed up the stairs, past Lulu's room, and let herself into the Chinese Suite. She started at the sound of Lulu's
dog yapping. Nothing seemed changed from her previous
visit. The boxes she had shoved under the bed when Winnie
appeared were as she had left them. She pulled out the first
box, took out the rolled-up canvas, and gently untaped it.
She stared at it for a moment. White and green, clusters of
water lilies. Lovely. She rolled it up again, very carefully,
hoping that she was not doing any damage. Hugh had given
it to Sylvie, but to whom did it really belong?

Margaret set off to find Winnie, the canvas under her arm.

Hugh's diaries might tell the truth, but where, oh, where
were they? Winnie might tell the truth, but when Margaret
knocked on her door, there was no answer. Of course she
had to try the door, and of course she entered when it opened.

"Winnie?" she whispered, afraid to startle the old woman
out of sleep. There was still no answer and no sign of Winnie. Margaret turned on the curious lamp and gazed about
the cluttered room, then looked again more closely. She could

not be mistaken: one thing she had noticed on her previous
visit was now missing.

Margaret felt she ought to locate Winnie, but she was now
so tired that her eyelids burned. She had been on the move
since Sunday morning and felt that she had never been so
tired in her life. She stumbled on the stairs leading from
Winnie's room, fighting exhaustion to try to find where Winnie might have gone: roaming about the big house, fluttering
about the gardens, stalking around the pool, gathering up
echoes of a past that couldn't have been all that joyful.

Then she sighed. A search of the house by someone who
didn't know the place was hopeless, and in any case, if Winnie was somewhere in the house, she was probably all right.

Margaret forced herself to make a brief tour of the grounds.
She circled the house as best she could, discovering dark
paths and murky shadows, which she avoided, plus outbuild-
ings and even a tennis court. It was too dark to see much,
but certainly there was no obvious sign of Winnie. At last
she found herself back at the pool, which was glowing faintly
blue from the lights at each end. Wearily, she opened the
door of her bungalow, turned on the lights, and stopped,
suddenly awake and tense. She sensed that someone had been
there in her absence. What was it? The packages from her
shopping tour were slightly rearranged. The pillows on the
bed were a bit rumpled, as though someone had felt under
them. She went into the unused bedroom and felt beneath
the mattress. The diaries and Winnie's memoirs were as she
had left them. She brought them into the other bedroom to
keep them and the rolled-up canvas at her side through the
night.

Margaret had barely undressed and fallen into bed before
she was deeply asleep.

When she awoke the next morning, the sun was touching
the windows of the bungalow. For a moment she didn't recognize where she was and then she knew. She would have to
rush to make her breakfast meeting with Charles Code, but
then she remembered that her car was still somewhere near
last night's restaurant. She flew to the shower and tried to
make herself reasonably glamorous for her meeting.

Millburne was found in the kitchen—a huge, old-fashioned room complete with a walk-in refrigerator that was opened by heavy wooden doors. It had not been altered since the heyday of Hugh Lonsdale. A large and elegant Mexican woman with her hair sleekly captured in a bun at the nape of her neck was placing cups and saucers on trays.

"Good morning, Millburne," Margaret said. "I am in something of a silly pickle. I have to meet Mr. Code at the Bel-Air Hotel for breakfast, but I have left my auto where I dined last night."

Millburne looked at his watch gravely and said, "Madame should not have any need for the Rolls this morning. The chauffeur is not in, but the boy will drive you. It would not be fitting for you to drive the Rolls yourself."

"Excellent," Margaret said. "I ought to leave soon, but I do not expect it to be a long meeting."

"Maria," Millburne said, "if Madame or Mrs. Lonsdale require their coffee, please see that the trays are taken up. I shall return when I have seen to Lady Margaret.

"We do not have a large live-in staff," Millburne explained as he led the way through the front door. "One of Madame's economies."

"I looked for Mrs. Lonsdale last night. She was not in her rooms."

"She wanders," Millburne said. "She manages to turn up when it's time for food, or preferably drink."

The Mexican boy was discovered raking the pebbles on the drive. In an instant, however, he had donned a stylish gray jacket and looked entirely presentable as a pickup chauffeur. He seemed to like the idea of driving the massive old Rolls.

The winding roads to the Bel-Air showed that quite a few early risers were speeding to power breakfasts about town. The Bel-Air was charmingly landscaped with pink buildings hidden away behind lush greenery. Margaret crossed a short bridge below which two decorative swans paddled in a peaceful pond. She passed along a pink-walled loggia to an outdoor restaurant precisely at eight, ready to meet Charles Code at last.

* * *

Lulu Lambert turned over heavily in her white-on-white bed, raised her sleep mask a fraction to note that the sun was up, and then decided to sleep on.

Kasparian woke early, too, in his comfortable suite and saw that the golden California sun was shining outside his windows. But the night had been extremely tiring, so it was not difficult for him to close his eyes again and drift into uneasy sleep.

Cherylle, in her big house, was cross. She could hear the two Code children quarreling as they were readied for school. Fuji had already brought the Mercedes around to drive them, so at least they would be out of her hair for the day. Cherylle was cross because Charles had come home very late—if indeed he had come home at all. Certainly he was nowhere to be found when she got up early to do her aerobics. When she had questioned Fuji, however, he had put on that irritating blank look, as though he didn't understand what she was saying, but he did, perfectly well. As soon as she and Charles were married, Fuji was out of here.

By the time Margaret was being helped from the Rolls at the Bel-Air, Debby Zahn was already on the road, talking on her car phone, cajoling, wheedling, promising the earth to the seller of one of the great houses in Holmby Hills to come on the market.

Donny Bright carefully styled his hair and adjusted his best Armani jacket. He was sure he had hooked Mrs. Marvin Smith as a client, and it was absolutely necessary that he find someone to replace Sylvie Code on Wednesdays. Life-style advising paid very well—but only if one had sufficient clients to advise.

Iris Metcalfe watched the early sun sparkling on the Pacific at Del Mar. The long sandy beach was almost deserted, and the waves that washed in from the other side of the world were very gentle. Then Iris entered a long black limousine that would take her to a mudpack and a massage in the quiet luxury of La Costa spa, followed by tennis with that attractive man who had told her he was staying the week.

Prince Paul Castrocani did not awake early, since he had barely found his bed before the sun began to rise.

Winnie Lonsdale, sunk into her deep bed of ivy, behind a thicket of ornamental shrubs, did not awaken at all.

As Millburne attended his butlerish duties, he noted that the pool man had arrived for his weekly visit and was lackadaisically scooping the floating leaves from the surface of the water. Millburne, however, did not see that the pool man had discovered a perfectly good, unopened bottle of vintage champagne left standing on the ground next to one of the cabanas. The pool man thought for exactly one minute, then decided that he worked hard for his few bucks and who would miss one bottle at a place like this? He put it in his carryall, and not much later the pool man was on his way to his next job.

Millburne summoned one of the maids at last and instructed her to look into Mrs. Lonsdale's rooms. It was uncommonly late for her to arise, although Millburne knew perfectly well that she had a habit of staying up until all hours to roam about her old house. Nevertheless, the cook wanted to clear away and get on with her shopping.

"Not there," the maid reported, drawing on her limited English. "*Ellá no dormió en su cama.* No sleep in bed."

Millburne rolled his eyes. Where had the woman got to? It meant he had to look in all of the many upstairs and downstairs rooms to find where Winnie Lonsdale had suddenly fallen asleep, tired out by that final glass of vodka. He started on the first floor. She had not decided to sleep in grandeur in the thronelike chair at the head of the endless table in the Versailles dining room. The little Spanish-style library was empty. She was not curled up near the mummy case in the Egyptian Suite. The door to the Chinese Suite was locked.

After he had searched upstairs and down, except for Lulu Lambert's rooms, he made his way to the cabanas beside the pool. There he found only the bitsy bathing costumes in readiness for the girls, who liked to oil themselves in the sun. Lady Margaret's bungalow was locked but was unlikely to harbor Winnie. The next bungalow's door was unlatched, but evidence of the recent visitors had been erased by the maids.

Millburne started along the path that led to a third bungalow, this only a seldom-used single-room structure with a little sitting porch. He stopped on the path when he caught sight of a bit of bluish chiffon almost buried under ivy. Then he stared and saw that beneath the gauzy strip of cloth was an outflung white hand. Winnie Lonsdale had been found.

Chapter 19

*M*argaret *confessed* to herself that she was somewhat apprehensive about meeting Charles Code, so she looked furtively at every man who entered. The women, she had to admit, were all beginning to look the same. Perhaps it was the fact of nearly identical noses.

Time passed, and still Charles did not arrive.

"Lady Margaret Priam?" a man asked.

She turned in her chair, prepared to face Charles at last, but this man was clearly an employee of the hotel.

"We have had a call. An English gentleman by the name of Millburne asks that you return to Mrs. Lambert's house as soon as possible. There has been a death."

Margaret stood up. Her immediate thought was that the rigors of dealing with Sylvie's murder and the long trip west had done Kasparian in.

"Did he say who . . . ?"

"No, ma'am. A death was all he said."

"I was expecting to meet a man named Charles Code," she said. "He is late, and I must go. Please explain."

"We know Mr. Code. We will inform him."

"Please hurry," Margaret said to the boy who was driving the Rolls. Then she summoned up her limited Spanish. *"Por favor, más rápido."*

The driver nodded, then set out to prove that the stately

old Rolls had power to spare. It careened around curves, passing four-wheeled youngsters that thought they were the lords of the road.

The gates to Lulu's estate were opened wide, and the drive in front of the house was filled with Beverly Hills police cars. The usually quiet house was in an uncommon uproar. The sounds of rapid Spanish came from the back of the house, and shrill voices, among them Lulu's, rang out from above. Then Paul appeared in a robe on the landing above the hall, looking bleary-eyed and unshaven. Margaret headed for him.

"What has happened? Is it Bedros?"

Paul shook his head. Then Kasparian appeared, looking confused and haggard. Margaret breathed a sigh of relief.

"Who, then?"

"Mrs. Lonsdale," Millburne said gravely from behind her. "Murdered." He did not look entirely displeased by the turn of events. "The police seem to think it might have been an intruder since the gates were unlocked. A boy ought to have been up and on watch until midnight, but he was watching television. Mrs. Lonsdale appears to have been wandering about near the bungalows and was struck by a heavy object. I regret to say that you were probably the last to see her alive."

"Where is Lulu?"

"She is discussing the situation with a man from the police," Kasparian said. "They will not say if it happened before Lulu and I went out, which means that . . ." He stopped.

"You are once again a possible murder suspect," Margaret finished for him.

"I do have a Lonsdale connection," Kasparian said.

Paul said, "I feel I need some coffee. I came back here at . . . I forget what the time was, but it seems like only a few hours ago. There are some quite amusing clubs if you know where to find them. The young ladies I was with knew very well."

"Come along, sir," Millburne said. "Mr. Kasparian looks as though he could use some sustenance as well."

The two men trailed after Millburne, and Margaret started

up to Lulu's rooms. On the landing she encountered the same young policeman with the fantastic teeth who had guided her to the Code house.

"Hello," he said. "I know you. You're the one looking for a murderer."

"That was at another house," Margaret said.

The young policeman frowned.

"Like a television series," Margaret said. "One week I look for a murderer here. The next week a murderer there."

The policeman nodded his understanding. Show business was more like real life than real life. She hoped he was too smart to accept that tale upon reflection, but it sent him on his way for the moment.

Lulu was wearing a remarkable lace peignoir, and her hair was wrapped in some wild contrivance designed to keep her multiple platinum curls in place. Either she slept in her makeup or she was a whiz at applying it rapidly in the face of an invasion by the police.

The man in civilian clothes who must be a detective was neither young nor handsome, but he seemed to know Lulu personally. He was introduced to Margaret as "a friend from the old days."

"It looks pretty routine," the detective said. "I've been giving Lulu hell for not keeping the gates locked. Why pay for all that private security when you're inviting the criminal element to walk right in?"

"Do you know how she was killed? A weapon or something?"

"Not a thing. Can't figure it out, but we're searching the grounds. Nothing was disturbed in the house. Some guy was probably looking the place over and this Lonsdale woman surprised him. Lulu tells me she had a habit of wandering around at night."

Margaret remembered that her rooms in the bungalow had been searched but too carefully to indicate a casual thief out to grab what was lying about. Although she did not care to bring up Sylvie, there was no question in her mind that the two deaths were linked. She was glad that she had hidden the diaries away again, along with the memoirs and the painting. It really was time to take a look at what Winnie had to say.

"I visited briefly with Mrs. Lonsdale in her room before I went out to dinner," Margaret said. "I did not see her when I returned." Should she mention that Winnie had not been in her rooms late last night? She should. "Although I did look for her. She was not about."

"You can never tell where Winnie will be," Lulu said. "Thinks this is still her house. Thought, I should say. I'll kind of miss her."

"Well, this will set the neighborhood in a state for a while," the detective said. "And we'll have a rash of dog bites." He saw that Margaret looked puzzled. "News of a murder gets around and people here get nervous, go out and buy attack dogs they don't know how to handle. Dog bites the hand that feeds it, that sort of thing." He stood up. "My men will be out of here soon. I'll probably have to ask a few more questions. And, Lulu, keep those damned gates locked, will you?"

"I have to be away for a day or two," Margaret said. "Will that be all right?"

"You pick up a boulder and knock her on the head? No? Then go. I can't see an English lady as a murderer."

"How reassuring," Margaret murmured. She wondered where Charles Code had been last night after dark.

Suddenly the glorious Beverly Hills day didn't seem as bright as it had when she first arrived in California. Perhaps it was the sight of two people from the police searching through the grounds. A patch of ivy on the path had been cordoned off with yellow plastic tape to mark the site of Winnie Lonsdale's end. Would she, Margaret wondered, rest near Hugh? Or was that reserved only for the gorgeous Sylvie?

Vague guilt was beginning to grow. If she had spent more time searching for Winnie the night before, could she have prevented her death? Might she at least have been close enough on the heels of the murderer to have known who it was?

She felt a definite need to be comforted. The temptation

to ring De Vere was very strong, but another murder—with both Margaret and Kasparian on the scene—would not please him, even if she denied any connection between the two events. She could try to explain the situation to the Beverly Hills police, but what kind of trouble would that cause without any specific end in view?

She went into her bungalow, which seemed chilly and gloomy, and rang Charles Code's office. Not unexpectedly, she was told that he was out but was expected back later. Peter Frost was not in. Margaret retrieved the diaries and the memoirs, but in spite of the dreary atmosphere of the bungalow, she decided not to make a public show of reading them beside the pool.

She picked up the volume of Hugh's diaries from the years immediately after the war. Even if the wartime diaries were in someone else's hands, she might get a sense of him or some hint of the past.

It was more than a hint. It was the whole story.

"I was lax for too long about doing more than jotting a few notes during the war," Hugh had written, "and perhaps my adventures will have no interest to posterity in any event."

Aha, Margaret thought. These were written with an eye to making them public one day. She read on.

As I fought the evil enemy with my friends of the French resistance, I could not but think what a grand film could be made. (Heard that Henry Hathaway has done a film with Cagney about the OSS in France, but my idea is better.) In Paris in '44 I ran into Bedros Kasparian, who had somehow managed to enter occupied France and was on the trail of a pile of paintings owned by René Zahn. I knew Zahn in the old days, before the war. Nice enough chap, although I did not know about the pictures that had been collected by his father and grandfather as well as himself, all stored away in that dreary old bourgeois house of his. A treasure trove. Bedros asked my help in getting the pictures and himself out of the country. Of course I agreed. But it went wrong. Kasparian never intended to pay for the pictures, that was clear, so he went to a man I had indicated was a collaborator and told him

that Zahn was a Jew, that he was active in the resistance.
Not true, the part about the underground, and whether he
was Jewish or not, I do not know. But Zahn was taken
before Bedros could get the pictures. I did help him out
of France, but with empty hands.

I did not tell anyone what Bedros had done. He is in
my debt forever. Greed will drive men to do extraordinary
things.

Margaret put down the diary. Poor Bedros. At least Hugh
had not known about Maurice Zahn in America, who would
long be supported by Kasparian's guilt.

She leafed through the rest of the diary but did not see
Kasparian's name mentioned again.

Greed, Margaret thought, was not a phenomenon only of
the dear, departed 1980s. Greed is eternal. She thought back
over her handful of years with Kasparian.

He was perfectly pleasant and courtly, an astute and apparently honest dealer in his chosen field. He lived well, if
Margaret was a judge of the well-tailored suits he wore at
the shop and their occasional expensive lunches and dinners
at fine restaurants where he was readily recognized by the
maître d's. The society ladies who visited the shop often
invited him to private gatherings. He rarely went. He was on
all of the lists for important charity events. He contributed
generously but usually gave away the tickets that permitted
one to mingle with people dressed to be seen and to dine on
poor food, however dramatically it was described by Poppy
Dill in her society column. There had been a Mrs. Kasparian
in the past, long before Margaret's time. She had no idea if
there were Kasparian offspring. All in all, she never thought
of Kasparian as greedy.

There was still the last diary of Hugh Lonsdale's life, the
one she had taken in the hope of finding out more about his
relationship with Sylvie.

"I have loved, made love to, too many women." The
precise script of the earlier diaries had become shakier as the
years overtook Hugh. The entries were short: references to
the days of past fame, the deaths of his Hollywood contem-

poraries, irritation about poor Winnie. It seemed that their
marriage, such as it was, had gone on so long that nothing
could ever break it. Not even the beautiful Sylvie, who suddenly appeared in the pages of the diary. "A nymph in the
pool, there before my eyes," he wrote. "Of all the nymphs
that frequent my pool—Lulu's pool now—this one, this Sylvie, brings back my distant youth, the memories. . . ."

Then, later, he wrote:

> I cannot say whether I am fascinated or repelled by
> Sylvie's dark-haired friend. A cheap little tart, but I rec-
> ognize the ambition. She will never be a star, but she
> seems so determined. She demands a steep price for her
> favors, and I believe that Lulu assists her in locating new
> conquests. Old habits die hard.

So much for Iris, the aspiring actress, starry-eyed and
innocent. Margaret wondered if Hugh Lonsdale's final infat-
uation had made him blind to Sylvie's character, while seeing
Iris's rather sharply.

Near the end of the diary, Hugh wrote, "I have given her
a little gift but warned her to keep it for some great emergency. The longer she keeps it, the more it will be worth."

The last pages of the diary were blank, but the final entries
were revealing.

> Bedros is here for a visit. He has done the unforgivable
> and introduced my Sylvie to a young lawyer who is quite
> taken with her. Taken her away, I should say. Is this the
> punishment that has been waiting in the wings for all these
> years for what I did? He is Charles Code, the grandson of
> René Zahn, whom I sent to his death.

Margaret paused and reread the sentence. Surely Hugh
had made a mistake. Surely he meant that Bedros had sent
René to his death during the war.

> For all these years [Hugh wrote] I have never failed to
> remind Bedros with cruel hints that I knew well that he
> had betrayed his friend Zahn by speaking unwisely to a

person the *résistants* knew to be a collaborator. Should I tell him now, as I suffer the loss of Sylvie, that it was I who informed on Zahn and I who managed to spirit away many of those paintings of the ''new masters'' from his house? At least I was able to live well thanks to them when my career failed. One of them even purchased an old man's last pleasure. She demanded the Renoir. It was not a good one, but genuine. Shall I tell Bedros? No. But it would have made a great film.

Margaret put down the diary. Sylvie had a Monet, Iris had acquired a Renoir. Who had the Renoir from Winnie's room?

Winnie's yellow pages were in direct opposition to her husband's flowery and romantic memories. In Winnie's hands the events of the recent past took on rather harsher tones: an old man pretending to be young, with a lecherous interest in the beautiful girl with the red-gold hair who may have had no more than a daughterly interest in him. A dark-haired adventuress who wanted to plunder what remained of value; the babes around Lulu's pool who played at having careers in films. Lulu herself presiding over the comings and goings of powerful, self-satisfied men who ran the companies in a company town, who paused at the legendary lady's house for a pleasant afternoon from time to time among lovely companions.

The sprawling handwriting was sometimes difficult to decipher, but Winnie had supplied what was almost certainly the answer to her death and, by extension, the answer to Sylvie Code's. There was one further bit of information Margaret needed, the answer to a question about the state of a marriage.

Dianne Stark, in her safe and luxurious multiroom Manhattan apartment, had not departed for the various weekday appointments so essential to the social swim when Margaret's call came through.

"Lucky you called when you did," Dianne said. "I was on my way to my regular volunteer hours. I am teaching a person to read, although whether he will end up enjoying

Shakespeare or simply the *New York Post* is a question I cannot yet answer. How is California treating you?''

"The past two days have been quite crammed with unlikely events. Sylvie Code's funeral in the reproduction of a Scottish church and a naked man taking a swim at a show-business party are but two of the highlights. And another murder.''

"Does murder follow you, or do you cause it to happen?''

"A bit of both, I'm afraid. Look, Dianne, I know you don't gossip—''

"Not much," Dianne said, "and then only in the nicest possible way.''

"How about rumors? I wonder if you've heard any rumors about a certain couple.''

When Margaret replaced the receiver, she had been informed of a number of rumors, all of which suggested that wealthy marriages had the same kinds of troubles as poor ones did. The only difference was that the clothes were much nicer for the rich. And in the larger marital abode there were many more doors to slam dramatically.

Chapter 20

*M*argaret put a few useful bits of clothing into a small overnight bag, found her rental car, which Lulu's boys had retrieved from the restaurant, and told Kasparian not to stir from Beverly Hills until she returned.

Paul looked somewhat improved with the aid of the coffee provided by Maria, the cook, and Millburne.

"I am going to settle this," Margaret said. "I am not going to ask you to come with me because you would report back to De Vere, and he would become highly incensed."

"What are you going to do, then?"

"I shall visit Charles Code, who has a rather good reason for not wanting me to see him face-to-face, and then I shall pamper myself grandly for a day."

"You will naturally be careful," Paul said, without much hope in his voice.

"Naturally," she replied. "It will all be very public, so there isn't much to be worried about."

Margaret drove to the massive accumulation of futuristic, outsized buildings that was Century City, rather an imitation of a city to the west of Beverly Hills.

Margaret proceeded down a broad roadway that seemed to be called the Avenue of the Stars, but few people, let alone stars, were in evidence. She plunged into a netherworld of complicated parking garages and briefly experienced a moment of terror upon leaving her car. Either she would be lost to the world forever among these rows and rows of gleaming autos or she would return to fetch her car and find herself roaming the concrete galleries through the years, growing older and paler, seldom catching sight of another human being.

Then she found her way to the surface, to be surrounded by awesome piles of glass, while whirls of wind swept across spaces that seemed designed for giants.

Charles Code's law firm was located in one of these gigantic towers. A silent elevator whisked her upward, the door opened, and she walked directly into a rich, rich office where the front desk was staffed by one of the glossiest young women she had seen in a town filled with gloss. Perfect hair and perfect nails, and a perfectly ingenious low-cut business suit from which the blouse had been omitted for a more provocative look.

"Charles Code, please," Margaret said.

"He's in conference," the young woman said. She had looked Margaret over and decided that she was not important.

"I must see him," Margaret said. "It's about his daughter's birthday party—and two murders. Tell him it's Lady Margaret Priam. I shall not leave until I have seen him."

"I'll have to check with his secretary." The meaning of grudging assent was defined in her reluctant agreement to place an internal call to the secretary of Charles Code. "She'll be out in a minute," the young woman told her. "Please take a seat."

The available seats were imaginative objects in earth-toned leathers that were probably the chairs of the future, grouped around a huge, low glass table balanced on some sort of granite boulder. A wall of potted plants with large notched leaves and spiky purple and red flowers formed a somewhat Rousseauesque backdrop. The magazines to read while cooling one's heels as one's attorney argued in his office on multilined phones about multimillion-dollar deals were *LA Style*, *Los Angeles*, and the current issues of *The Hollywood Reporter* and *Daily Variety*. But no, of course the big, big stars wouldn't wait here. The not-so-big and the very small would wait, and the bothersome pokers into other people's lives like Margaret would wait and wait even longer.

Her point was proved by the dramatic entrance of a woman who was Really Famous and looked it. Margaret could not immediately identify her, but she caused the receptionist to spring to her feet and fawn. The Star's entourage of well-muscled men (possibly armed) and bustling assistants met a phalanx of secretaries who poured out from the inner offices and escorted the Star to her destination.

Margaret waited, then waited some more. Charles Code was not going to escape her this time, unless, like Winnie, he knew a back way out.

"Lady Margaret?"

Margaret looked up from reading about current movie grosses in *The Hollywood Reporter*.

The voice was familiar—she had spoken enough to Charles on the phone and had heard him speaking to Lulu. And it didn't surprise her to realize, now that she looked straight at him, that she had seen him before, more than once.

"I am so glad to meet you at last. I was told at the Bel-Air that you had been called away by a sudden death?" He raised his voice in a question, as though sudden death was an unfamiliar concept to him. He was smooth, he was tanned, he was quite satisfied with his life. He didn't look the least bit guilty about anything.

"Yes," Margaret said, and stood up. "Winnie Lonsdale. She was found dead on the grounds of Lulu Lambert's house."

"Forgive me for saying so, but she was a tiresome old woman whom most people felt the urge to silence from time to time."

"Do you think someone silenced her, then?" Margaret asked sweetly. "A lot of that going on."

"Why don't we go into my office?" Charles said.

Although she was fairly certain that Charles Code didn't represent any kind of irreversible danger, she was glad to see that he left his door slightly ajar so that his secretary, in her splendid situation, was within the sound of Margaret's voice.

"I must seem highly evasive to you," Charles said, "but it has been a difficult time personally and professionally. You were so very kind to accompany Sylvie's ashes. I was late getting to the church yesterday for the funeral—"

"That is a pleasant fiction," Margaret said, "but I don't believe you. Did you not refer to me as 'Not stupid . . . Even if she is English,' well before most of the mourners had arrived?"

"I don't think . . ." Now he did have the good grace to look somewhat chagrined. "I didn't mean to imply—"

"No matter," Margaret said. "I am brighter than I look, even on a spring day in Manhattan after having viewed the body of a murdered woman. I say, I understand that you hope to acquire Lulu Lambert's property one day, to tear down the old house and build anew."

"It was originally Sylvie's idea. She had delusions of grandeur. She was terribly greedy and terribly acquisitive. After we started to talk divorce, I decided that I was going to go ahead with that house if I could persuade Lulu to sell, just to spite Sylvie. My ex-wife is negotiating with Lulu. I suppose you find that strange."

"Not any longer," Margaret said. "Shall Cherylle then become the lady of the house if your plans come to reality?"

Charles Code actually laughed. "Not likely. I understand you've met Cherylle. What do you think? She isn't a bad person, but Sylvie probably talked a lot of viciousness to you about Cherylle."

"For the final time, I will say that I barely knew your wife. I don't care for the idea that she used me as an excuse for her activities of ferrying art objects to New York for Kasparian and in indulging in the odd bit of blackmail. That was probably what triggered her murder, to your good fortune, since there is now no expensive divorce settlement."

"Mmmm." Charles seemed distracted. "It doesn't matter now, does it? I admit Sylvie's death was financially beneficial to me, and what difference does it make who did it? I don't suppose it was Kasparian. My mother claims he couldn't do such a thing, that he was a saint. Well, I got tired of that. My whole life he's made a point of reminding me that he paid for my schooling and my father's before me. Anyhow, she's dead. It was probably one of your New York drug addicts who broke in.''

"I think you know it wasn't," Margaret said, "although perhaps you don't care to admit that. I am sure the police will discover that you were there in New York when she was murdered and not in California at all. In fact, you were there for a day or so after. Rather suspicious.''

He did not deny his presence in New York, but he did say, "I did not kill Sylvie. Peter Frost is a better bet. He was in New York, too, and I wouldn't put it past Sylvie to have been double-crossing him. If Peter wants this firm, he's going to have to buy me out at a very, very high price.''

"I'd hate to think that Peter murdered her—and Winnie Lonsdale. I suppose the authorities will get around to asking you where you were last night when Winnie was killed.''

"I was dining with a business associate," Charles said. "I went home early. Ask Cherylle.''

"I could do that," Margaret said, "but it's unnecessary. I know that you were at Marvin Smith's house for his party, and quite a lot of other people know that as well.''

"Winnie Lonsdale was a bore, but how often do bores get what is coming to them? I had no reason to kill that dreary old dame.''

"Someone had a reason," Margaret said. "It was roughly the same reason Sylvie was murdered.''

"And who would that be?" Charles leaned forward in his chair and challenged Margaret with a look.

"You know," she said. "Or at least you suspect. Now, you will come to little Alexandra's birthday party on Saturday. I shall stay on until that evening. I warn you that I shall insist that both Debby and Cherylle come. Sylvie left the plans in good order.''

"I'll come," Charles said. He seemed relieved that the subject was no longer murder. "If they don't have me in jail.''

"Never fear," Margaret said. She stood up. "I'm glad to meet you at last.''

"How did you reach the conclusion that I was in New York when Sylvie was murdered?" Charles asked.

"First, it seemed logical. Kill the wife and save the divorce settlement. Then I saw you there. At Iris Metcalfe's house, the day after. You were leaving. I didn't know it was you, of course, and I couldn't figure out why you were so elusive about seeing me out here. Then I caught sight of you again briefly at Lulu's house, although I won't explain how, and realized that you thought I might recognize you. I came round today to be sure. I'm surprised you didn't flee."

"It's too late for that," he said. "I know what you're thinking about the murders, but I don't think you can prove anything."

"We'll see," Margaret said. "I look forward to your attendance on Saturday. Bring a nice gift."

She left him sitting at his desk.

"Could you show me out?" she said sweetly to his secretary. "So stupid of me, but I can't remember the way to the elevators."

When Margaret and the secretary reached the reception desk, Margaret paused. "Thank you so much. I can find my way."

The receptionist marked her place in the magazine she was reading and looked up at Margaret blankly. Perhaps so many titled people passed through the firm's doors that she simply couldn't keep them straight.

"Is Peter Frost in?"

"No," the receptionist said shortly. "He's out of town for a couple of days."

"If he calls in, could you tell him that Lady Margaret has gone south for a few days of healthy spa activity? I'll ring him when I get back. Thank you so much."

The receptionist looked as though she agreed that poor, old Lady Margaret could use some toning and beautifying. Margaret thought that one day the receptionist would have to face the fact of being thirty-five and then she'd be sorry she hadn't been kinder.

Chapter 21

*H*appily, *Margaret* spent only fifteen to twenty minutes trying to locate her car in the underground parking garage. Since it was an unfamiliar car at that, she came upon several she thought were hers before finding the right one.

She ventured onto the San Diego Freeway with some trepidation. The steady flow of cars heading south was briefly terrifying, but she decided that if several million Angelinos could manage it, so could one displaced Brit. Once she had merged with the flow, she found that as long as she followed the rules and kept moving, the problems sorted themselves out. She turned on the car radio to a "lite" music station, settled back, and simply allowed the scene to pass.

Since the freeways were elevated ribbons of concrete with occasional dramatic curving ramps, she was able to view the city on either side, fairly closer at hand now than it had been at night from a distant hillside in the Hollywood Hills. As she drove away from the center of the city, she marveled at the massive numbers of people who must live on either side of the multilane highway, so many that it was hard to see how they had deluded themselves into believing they were living in suburbia.

She resisted the strong temptation to leave the freeway and head for the coast and places named Corona del Mar, Laguna Beach, and Capistrano Beach, but she pressed on, passing through San Juan Capistrano and San Clemente. The Pacific was out there, blue and serene on this warm spring day, and the surfers and bathers were strewn along the beaches.

Off the freeway at last, Margaret drove cautiously, following her map inland until she arrived at La Costa Hotel and Spa and proceeded up the picture-perfect road bordered by manicured lawns and masses of colorful flowers. Expensive-looking condominiums were to one side and the grand spa complex to the other. The rolling green golf course to her right was dotted with afternoon foursomes, and at the tennis courts fit, tanned players engaged in serious matches.

She came to a stop in a wide area between two large low buildings and allowed herself to be helped from the car with devastating politeness by a hotel attendant.

"I have only a bit of luggage," she said. "I may not be staying. Could you see to the car until I've decided?"

The building that housed the lobby was cool and light and low-key. A few women in tennis outfits awaited partners in the lobby chairs, and off to one side a shop displayed many shelves filled with bottles of pastel-colored beauty products.

"I have not booked a room," Margaret said to the young man at the reception desk, "but I had hoped to stay the night. Lady Margaret Priam. I am here to see Iris Metcalfe."

"We are pretty full," the man said. "Let me see." He came up with one. "It's in this building, only a double, I'm afraid. The suites are all booked."

"That will be fine," Margaret said, as she signed her name to the credit-card receipt. "I wonder if someone could track Mrs. Metcalfe down. It's rather urgent."

The young man at the desk was doubtful. One did not intrude unnecessarily on the guests at a world-famous spa and hotel where people were intent on getting away from it all, not having the world track them down. He took Margaret's measure, then apparently decided that she was not the law, not a madwoman, and not a vengeful spouse or an irate girlfriend.

"I will ring her suite," he said. But naturally Iris was not there, not with spa treatments and golf courses and tennis courts abounding.

"I'll look about for her," Margaret said, "after I am settled."

In short order Margaret found herself in a room large enough to house at least one of New York's homeless families. She reviewed the bottled mineral water, the multiple types of soaps, the shampoos and conditioners, and the other amenities in the bath, then read through the literature that provided directions to the various activities throughout the complex. When she had her bearings, she went out in search of Iris.

Iris was not at the spa being mudpacked, massaged, or Jacuzzied. She was not eating a healthy snack or taking a dip in the spa pool. She might have been somewhere off on a golf course, but Margaret failed to imagine Iris as an avid golfer or even as much of a tennis player. Nevertheless, she strolled down to the rows and rows of tennis courts where earnest beginners practiced their serves and backhands under the watchful eye of a pro, while the experts volleyed with gusto in the late-afternoon sun. Iris was not there.

Margaret walked back up the incline from the courts to the main buildings. In the one across from the lobby was a collection of restaurants and lounges and the promise of choice shops for the impulse buyer on holiday. But Iris was not enjoying a solitary cocktail or an early meal, or trying on a beaded sweater with a substantial price tag.

If she remembered the map, up past the main buildings was an outdoor swimming pool and beyond it a cluster of buildings that offered more secluded luxurious guest rooms and suites. She looked down from her elevated position at artfully designed rocks and pools where large Japanese koi were swimming lazily. A few people reclined on lounges at the pool, heedless of the danger of suntanning. Some youngsters were splashing in the shallow end of the pool, and there in the shade reclining on a lounge was Iris, her hair wrapped in a turban and very large sunglasses covering her eyes.

Margaret took a deep breath, then joined her.

Iris appeared to be dozing. Margaret carried a chair from one of the tables and set it down at her side.

"Iris," she said quietly. "I'm surprised to find you still here."

Iris shook herself awake, swung her legs over the side of the chaise, and stared at Margaret.

"What on earth? What are you doing here?"

"You know me," Margaret said, "always looking for a chance to improve my well-being. And the chance to look into the odd murder or two."

"I don't know what you mean." Iris started to gather up her bag, her towel, the bottle of sunscreen, the jeweled thongs, the gauzy coverup.

"I mean bicoastal murders and some valuable bits of art. Not to mention some damaging personal history and your marriage to Horton Metcalfe, which seems to be running into difficulties. Not to mention again the other man and the other woman, depending on whose view you take."

"I am not going to listen to this," Iris said, and stood up. In her few years of involvement with New York high society, Iris had managed to perfect the tone of "Surely you know who I am," which lay behind every statement of outraged dignity.

"Sit down, Iris. I'm going to get the answers."

"I have nothing to say," Iris said, but she sat.

"Is this how it happened? Sylvie was always a danger to you because she knew about or shared your semiprofessional past as a good-time girl in Hollywood. Since you mentioned blackmail, perhaps she was blackmailing you to keep your past history from your highly respectable Horton. Or maybe she was planning to deal in dramatic revelations once she had come into her millions via her divorce."

"Horton is a most understanding man," Iris said.

"Rumor has it that he is not. Then there's Charles Code. An attractive man, don't you think? And probably more understanding than Horton. If Charles were free of Sylvie and Horton dumped you, Charles would be available. Except, of course, that damned divorce money."

"Very imaginative," Iris said.

"For a time I thought Charles must have murdered his wife. A really sound way to preserve one's capital. But it occurred to me that it's not all that easy to take a gun across the country through airport security. It isn't that easy for an out-of-towner to buy a gun once he's arrived. And even the best of friends don't loan guns to commit murder lest they be traced back. Then there were those alleged diaries. Were they really about Kasparian, or were they about you?''

"This is all nonsense," Iris said, "and to think that I was considering bringing you into my very nice social circle."

"Did Sylvie promise to hand over the diaries to you now that her future seemed sufficiently prosperous? Did you meet her at Kasparian's shop, having already decided that she could still talk even if she did give you the diaries?"

"If you repeat any of this to anyone, I shall sue," Iris said. She stood up again, and this time she seemed determined to depart.

"I haven't gotten to Winnie Lonsdale," Margaret said. "She knew the same things Sylvie did. And you borrowed the black car with tinted windows that Charles's firm leases to scare her, if not to kill her. Then the memoirs started to become reality. You were staying at the other bungalow at Lulu's but Lulu doesn't talk. If Winnie was safely disposed of and silenced for good . . .''

Iris stalked away toward the detached villas on the other side of the pool, at the edge of the golf course.

"I know about the paintings," Margaret said to her back. "I have the one Hugh Lonsdale gave to Sylvie. You must have the one that was in Winnie's room. Another Renoir looted from a man in France during the war? Did you promise to pay for it, but killed her instead?"

Iris did not turn back.

Margaret had done her best, even if Iris didn't admit to anything. She must have driven through the night last night to be here in the morning. What to do now? The local police would think she was bonkers if she tried to explain. The Beverly Hills police? That would take a long time explaining. New York was too many thousands of miles away.

It couldn't have been anyone but Iris, but it looked as though she was likely to get away with it. Horton Metcalfe, however dissatisfied he might be with his marriage to Iris, would use every bit of power at his command to suppress any kind of scandal. If Charles suspected Iris's guilt, he would keep quiet—the possibility of becoming a suspect himself, or at least part of a conspiracy, was too strong. Margaret was the only continuing danger for Iris, but what could she prove? Unless . . .

Margaret went back to the lobby and consulted with the concierge. Then she went to her room and rang through to Iris's suite.

"Don't hang up," she said. "Now that you know what I know, perhaps we can arrange something."

"I have nothing to say to you," Iris said. "I'm leaving for New York in the morning." Then, "Arrange what?"

"Iris darling, you know how expensive life in New York City is. And I do like my little comforts. Perhaps we could come to some agreement about, well . . . silence, let's call it."

Iris didn't speak for a moment.

"The only thing is," Margaret said, "I don't think it would be wise to be seen about this place together. I understand that there's a rather charming restaurant in Del Mar twenty minutes or so away. Jake's. It's right on the beach."

"I know it," Iris said shortly. "Across from the train station."

"I'll meet you there at nine," Margaret said. "Can you find your way?"

"I have a car and driver at my disposal," Iris said grandly. "Naturally. We'll be alone then."

"Just the two of us," Margaret said. "We can talk."

Jake's jutted out onto the long, flat beach at Del Mar. Alongside it a grassy slope with benches for viewing the ocean eased its way down to the sand. Margaret arrived in good time and found the restaurant quite full. As she waited at the bar tensed up with apprehension about what Iris might confess to—or agree to—she watched the patrons come and go from their dinners. A good many seemed to be highly prosperous older people, with the look of ones who might once have been famous and were not retired even from futile appearances at the Polo Lounge.

Iris was late, but that was to be expected. When she finally arrived, she was still wearing dark glasses and an elaborate arrangement of scarves in lieu of a turban. They were seated out in the glass-enclosed dining area right over the beach. It was almost dark, but there was a moon and enough light to see the waves rolling in.

"How much do you want?" Iris asked.

"Half the proceeds from the Renoir?"

"I still don't know what you are talking about."

"Did you take it from Winnie's rooms after she was dead, or was she bringing it to you? She told me she was coming into a lot of money and that she had an appointment." Margaret was not finding it easy to pose as a blackmailer. She could imagine the tension if one were actually trying to extract money from someone with a guilty secret.

"When I stayed at Lulu's place a few years ago," Iris said, "I couldn't bear the sight of that wicked old woman creeping around prying into everything, none of it any of her business."

"I suppose a wife, even one on a cranky footing with her husband, likes to keep track of him. I understand that Hugh was very fond of Sylvie."

Iris tossed her head and the scarves slipped down around her shoulders. "He fancied me, to tell the truth. These old men . . ."

"Fancied you enough to buy your goodwill with the remains of a fortune?"

"It is not a good picture," Iris said. "The other one is much better."

Then she stopped and her eyes met Margaret's. Margaret smiled.

"I can't bear this place any longer." Iris was on her feet. The waiter rushed over to see what the problem was. "I need air," she said. "Clear this away. Here." She handed the waiter a roll of bills.

"We haven't finished," Margaret said.

"I have," Iris said. "Come along. We'll talk on the beach.

Anyplace away from all these people." She slipped her large bag over her shoulder and walked through the restaurant out into the parking lot. Margaret followed. Iris strode ahead of her along the edge of the road, then turned onto the grass. Soon she was a distant figure on the sand in the deepening darkness. The *whoosh* and *thud* of the big waves hitting the beach were the only sounds.

Margaret hurried to catch up with her.

They were alone with the sand stretching to the right and to the left. The lights of Jake's were far away and the ocean was a black plain from which the waves rose and fell.

"Iris . . ."

"It was working out perfectly," Iris said over her shoulder. "Who could imagine I would shoot an old friend like Sylvie? No one knew about Charles and me."

"I knew. I saw him at your house the day after the murder. I knew you were in Los Angeles, at Sylvie's funeral, at the Polo Lounge, at Lulu's house."

"I can't lose what I've managed to get," Iris said. "I won't. Let Kasparian hang. Or Charles. She said she had Hugh's diaries, but what could Hugh have said? She did blackmail Kasparian, I know it. But for me it was what Sylvie could have said. I would always have to face that."

"It's not so terrible, you know," Margaret said. "Lots of people have what is called 'a past.' People know about it, and life goes on."

"It wouldn't have gone on for me," Iris said. "Not the way I wanted it to. Now there's you."

"But if I say nothing? And who would believe me?"

"You will make someone believe you. You would if you had the chance."

Margaret was not prepared to be attacked, and certainly not by a wealthy society lady suddenly wielding a very large bottle of the very best mineral water thoughtfully provided to the spa's guests.

Large shoulder bags can conceal the most amazing things, Margaret thought as the bottle struck at the side of her head. She managed to avert her head just enough so that the bottle hit her cheek. She gasped at the sharp pain and tried to wrench the bottle from Iris's hand.

Stupid, no! Margaret's dazed mind told her. Get away.

But sand is not made for running in fancy summer shoes. The pain was growing, but at least she was conscious. Still, she could not seem to make her feet carry her away.

Iris swung again, but Margaret dropped to the ground and the bottle arced through the empty air. Margaret rolled toward Iris and grabbed her legs. She lost her balance and toppled backward. Margaret stood up groggily and backed away from her.

Iris was unstoppable. She scrambled to her feet and brandished the bottle.

"I want it all," she said—it was more like a shriek. "All."

Then she was running, stumbling toward the grass and the road. Margaret was too dazed to follow quickly. But slowly and painfully she walked after Iris.

Her last sight of Iris was a disheveled woman waving wildly to someone down the road that paralleled the train tracks. A big black limousine drew up and Iris threw herself into the backseat and the car sped away.

Margaret touched her cheek gently. She wondered if the blow had broken a bone. At least it had not smashed her skull. When she examined her face in the mirror of her car, she found that she did not look terribly damaged. She hoped she would be able to drive herself back to the hotel.

She managed it, by driving very, very slowly and by repeating to herself: "I shall reach the hotel. I shall have a doctor summoned. I shall be all right."

"Ma'am, are you all right?" The boy who opened the car door at the hotel looked aghast. Perhaps she looked worse than she thought.

"I think not," Margaret said. "I . . ."

The boy caught her as she collapsed.

"Margaret, can you hear me?"

Margaret opened her eye. The other one seemed to have

been covered with a bandage. She could see that she was in her hotel room. The lights were turned very low.

"Yes, but who are you?"

She turned her head painfully. Peter Frost was sitting beside her bed.

"Peter! What are you doing here?"

"I was in San Diego on business and the office told me you had gone south to a spa. I thought I'd surprise you. But you surprised me."

"I didn't think anyone would believe me about Iris."

"Hmmm. If this is what Iris did to you, it seems to be some indication of the lengths to which she will go."

"Oh, she murdered Sylvie and Winnie. She wanted to keep her socially connected husband, and keep Charles, and get all the money she could, and . . ." Margaret touched her cheek. "Is it awful?"

"There was a doctor who thinks not but suggests that you be conveyed to a specialist for further consultation. I intend to do that in the morning."

"But what about Iris?"

"According to the hotel, early this evening Mrs. Metcalfe paid her bill, packed up her belongings, and notified her driver—not someone on the hotel's staff—that she was on her way to Mexico."

"Good Lord, do you mean to say that Iris has fled the country?"

"It seems that way, but I don't know that Tijuana, Ensenada, and the remote stretches of Baja, California will provide her with the ambience she is accustomed to. And there's a question of money."

"She has a painting that's worth quite a bit. *Quite* a bit."

"Again, the value of the *peso* being what it is. And I don't know that there are many art collectors hanging about the cactus patches."

"Greed is eternal," Margaret murmured. "I ought to explain all this to someone in authority."

"We will handle it," Peter said. "Don't forget I'm a lawyer."

"I think," Margaret said, "that Quintus Roach will definitely be interested in the story rights."

The last thing she thought as she fell into a deep sleep was that Peter Frost was a rather nice fellow, but De Vere was nicer, even though she could imagine how furious he'd be when she told him about this adventure.

Chapter 22

*P*aul, *however,* had the first opportunity to express his dismay, in rather strong terms.

"You are *pazza*. Crazy. Why didn't you take me with you? I could have protected you from this madwoman."

"I'm certain she would have run without saying anything if we'd both turned up. Promise you won't say a word to De Vere before I have a chance to explain."

"I think you were doing something not legal," Paul said.

"Too late now to worry about that," Margaret said. "I have to talk to Kasparian. You ought to be there, too."

Lulu herself had sniffed at the outline of the tale of Iris and her murders.

"Never expected anything better of her," Lulu said. "They'll catch her. A couple of weeks in Mexico are all well and good, but when you start thinking that those weeks are going to stretch out forever and ever, you plan your comeback. Half of you New Yorkers are certifiably nuts, so she can claim insanity and everyone will just shrug and say they knew it all along. Mark my words."

Margaret, Paul, and Kasparian met again beside Lulu's pool, and Margaret explained. "Bedros, you've been carrying a load of guilt for something you never did," she said. "Your chum Hugh Lonsdale betrayed Maurice's father and stole some of the pictures. It wasn't much of a problem to smuggle them out of France, even under the conditions of the occupation.'' She handed him Hugh's last diary. ''It's yours. It will explain.''

Then she handed him the rolled-up canvas she had found in Sylvie's Chinese Suite. ''Technically, this probably belongs to Charles since they were still married. I only looked at it briefly. It might be a Monet—water lilies, of course. Or it might be worthless.''

''Thank you,'' Kasparian said. ''I suppose there will still be a lot of police business to deal with, but I am glad to know how the parts fit together.'' He was looking even older and more tired. ''I'll see that it's yours one day.''

''I don't need it,'' Margaret said. ''Truly. Let it take care of you in your golden years. Oh, dear, I'm forgetting. Donny Bright is coming round to help out about the birthday party on Saturday. He's fitting me in among his clients. Happily, he has stated strongly that the monkey is out.''

''I was not planning to stay around to see it in any case,'' Paul said. ''Kasparian and I return to New York in the morning. I have one more night to enjoy the company of the young ladies I have met. There is a club that all the great young stars of today and tomorrow frequent. I would like to converse with Madonna. She is Italian, and I know how to speak to Italian women.''

''Not that one, I think,'' Margaret said under her breath. ''Neither of you will say a word to De Vere. I rang him yesterday and told him that I would be in New York on Sunday. I believe the damage to my face will be mended.''

Paul and Kasparian shook their heads.

''We will be silent,'' Paul said. ''Otherwise, De Vere will turn his anger on us.''

''It is all turning out well,'' Peter Frost said. Sixteen expensively dressed children were cavorting with a pack of clowns, while the After-Five Fantasies people lugged out a pink-frosted three-tiered cake decorated with marzipan rosebuds, butterflies, and silver-winged fairies.

''Little Alexandra seems happy,'' Margaret said. ''Charles

seems happy, Cherylle is reasonably happy, and Debby is on the brink of receiving a commitment from Lulu to sell, so she is delighted.''

"I suppose you are definitely leaving tomorrow," Peter said.

"Absolutely. California living is far too strenuous for me."

"I am in New York quite often," he said. "And there is nothing to keep you from traveling west from time to time."

The baby rock band began playing a raucous tune that Alexandra Code's seven-year-old guests appeared to enjoy immensely.

"No," Margaret said slowly. "Nothing much. Do call me when you next come to Manhattan."

Lulu sailed onto the horizon in a glittery, spangled dress not exactly suitable for an afternoon birthday party. Possibly she fancied herself as the good fairy. The nannies who had brought some of the guests gaped at the sight and whispered among themselves, but the handful of mothers merely smiled at her indulgently and put their heads back together to trade the latest gossip. Donny Bright, she noted, was circling around them, ready to make another life-style-advisor connection. Margaret even caught sight of Fuji standing alone far away from the pool, smiling benevolently on Alexandra's happy day.

Millburne passed among the children, offering champagne glasses full of bubbly pink punch. Since the burden of Winnie Lonsdale had been lifted, he appeared to be positively buoyant. Perhaps Quintus Roach was in need of an authentic English butler for an upcoming screen epic. . . . Margaret caught herself. Around here, show business insinuated itself effortlessly into one's thinking.

Margaret wandered among the noisy, frenetic children. Even Beverly Hills youngsters were apparently not so blasé as one might expect. Many of them were digging into enormous sundaes being dished out at an ice-cream wagon manned by a person dressed in a lion suit. Lulu had allowed a small pony, slightly dejected in its bejeweled bridle, to be tethered beyond the pool area for short rides and photos.

When Lulu's dog had taken offense at the sight of this animal in its territory, it had been banished to the house.

Alexandra Code at least had found that dreams do come true. She was seated on a sort of pink throne with a silver crown on her head, surrounded by piles of wrapping paper and bows and some very expensive gifts. What would she expect next year? And what would young Dorian Code demand for his next birthday?

Charles Code was watching his daughter breathlessly tear the wrapping from a package that contained a party dress that looked as though it had cost a fortune. And Margaret had merely given her a pretty little doll with blond braids and a gingham dress. What did she know about Beverly Hills children?

"Charles," Margaret said, "I ought to say good-bye since I'll be gone in the morning. It has been resolved, although not necessarily to the good of all."

Charles Code shrugged. "I bear a lot of the blame," he said. "I fancied Iris a bit even back when I first met Sylvie, but she had a rather acquisitive agenda that didn't appeal to me in the long run. Peter explained enough about what she did, so I get the picture, but I don't want to know a lot more until the law has its chance."

"It's been interesting," Margaret said. "I don't suppose we'll meet again soon."

"Likely not," he agreed. He hesitated. "I had a talk with Kasparian," he said finally. "He told me a few things about the past that I hadn't known. What he did for me and my father and why. When you get back to New York, would you have a chance to see my parents? Tell them how their grandchildren are. Maybe explain better than I could what all this business has been about." He shrugged. "Maybe it will make them think better of me. I'm too much a part of all this." He flung out an arm that took in Hugh Lonsdale's estate, which surely would be acquired by Charles someday, and the expensive lawns and palm trees of Beverly Hills, and beyond it all the freeways and hillsides and reflecting sky-scrapers of Los Angeles.

"I'll see them," Margaret said, and did not believe that their opinion of their son would change much.

The afternoon was fading, and the parents and nannies began to gather up their charges. The blue of the sky was paler, and the palm trees were dark silhouettes.

"It looks like a postcard," Margaret murmured. Then she corrected herself. "An exact reproduction of a postcard."

"What?" Charles asked.

"Nothing," Margaret said. "I was wondering aloud if spring had finally, really come to Manhattan."

About the Author

JOYCE CHRISTMAS has written six previous novels: *Hidden Assets* (with Jon Peterson), *Blood Child*, *Dark Tide*, *Suddenly in Her Sorbet*, *Simply to Die For*, and *A Fête Worse Than Death*. In addition, she has spent a number of years as a book and magazine editor. She lives in a part of New York City where as yet Society rarely sets foot.